You're invited to a

CREEPOVER ®

It Spells Z-O-M-B-I-E!

written by P. J. Night

SIMON SPOTLIGHT
New York   London   Toronto   Sydney   New Delhi

SIMON SPOTLIGHT
An imprint of Simon & Schuster Children's Publishing Division
1230 Avenue of the Americas, New York, New York 10020
First Simon Spotlight paperback edition July 2017
Copyright © 2017 by Simon & Schuster, Inc.
All rights reserved, including the right of reproduction in whole or in part in any form.
SIMON SPOTLIGHT and colophon are registered trademarks of Simon & Schuster, Inc.
YOU'RE INVITED TO A CREEPOVER is a registered trademark of Simon & Schuster Inc.
Text by Ellie O'Ryan
For information about special discounts for bulk purchases, please contact Simon & Schuster Special Sales at 1-866-506-1949 or business@simonandschuster.com.
Designed by Nick Sciacca
Manufactured in the United States of America 0617 OFF
10 9 8 7 6 5 4 3 2 1
ISBN 978-1-5344-0082-5
ISBN 978-1-5344-0083-2 (eBook)
This book has been cataloged with the Library of Congress.

CHAPTER 1

Emily Evans leaned close to the mirror, holding her breath in an attempt to be perfectly still. With a long, graceful swoop she dusted sparkly silver eye shadow onto her eyelids. She paused, blinked, and stared at her reflection. *Not bad,* she thought. *And if a little is good . . .*

Emily reached for a powder brush and dusted more eye shadow on her face—her cheeks, her forehead, her nose, everywhere. It was Halloween, after all, the best day of the year for crazy makeup—and crazy fun! Emily had been planning her costume for weeks. It was her first Halloween since she and her mom had moved to Riverdale, and Emily couldn't wait to go trick-or-treating with her new friends Abby Miller, Leah Rosen, and

Nora Lewis. At last, the big day was finally here. In just a few minutes, Emily would walk over to Abby's house for trick-or-treating and the best sleepover ever!

"Knock, knock!"

Emily made a face as her mom's voice carried through the closed bathroom door. She always did that—called out "Knock, knock," instead of just knocking like a normal person. It didn't used to bother Emily that much, but now it drove her kind of crazy.

"Almost done, Mom," Emily called back.

"Can't wait to see you in costume, Alien Queen!" Mom replied.

Emily did one more check in the full-length mirror. Her reflective silver tunic sparkled in the bright lights of the bathroom vanity. On every inch of skin—hands, arms, face, even neck—she had smeared a thick green makeup base. The silver eye shadow on top made her sparkle every time she moved! But Emily's favorite part of her costume was her hair. She had twisted it into a dozen braids, then sprayed each one with enough glitter hair spray to make them stand straight out from her head. Her shiny braids looked awesome, like razor-sharp tentacles.

And now, for the very last part of Emily's costume . . .

She carefully placed a gleaming metallic tiara on her head. It was a little wobbly, but Emily resolved to be careful. Besides, the glitter spray had made her hair feel really sticky. Hopefully it would help the tiara stick too.

Emily took a deep breath, then flung open the bathroom door. "Ta-da!" she cried as she struck a pose with one arm held high.

Mom beamed. "Oh, Emily! Look at you!" she exclaimed. "Take me to your leader!"

"Hey, that's my line!" Emily joked.

"I can't wait to post a picture of you!" Mom replied, fumbling for her phone.

Emily stood against the wall and made a scowling face.

"No, honey, *smile*," Mom urged her. "You look so pretty when you smile!"

"I'm an alien queen orchestrating a hostile take-over. Why would I smile?" Emily pointed out.

"Just one? For Grandma and Grandpa?" Mom pleaded.

Emily sighed, then made a giant, toothy grin. It was a totally sarcastic smile, but Mom didn't seem to notice as she took about a billion pictures with her phone.

"Look at your hair, defying gravity!" Mom marveled. "How'd you get it to stick out like that?"

"Half a bottle of extra-hold gel and four cans of glitter hair spray," Emily replied.

Mom's smile faded. "That much?" she asked, sounding worried. "But honey, that's going to be very hard to wash out! It could take days!"

Emily shrugged—but inside she felt a twinge of panic. She hadn't thought about that before. What if she had to go to school on Monday looking like this? Even worse— what if it took *weeks* for her hair to get back to normal?

"Too late to worry about it now," Emily said, putting her fears aside. "Anyway, I've gotta go. I don't want to hold up trick-or-treating."

"Have a great time," Mom said, trailing after Emily down the hall. "Are you sure you don't want a ride?"

Emily's overnight bag, sleeping bag, and pillow were already waiting by the front door. "Nope," Emily replied as she scooped everything into her arms. "I've got it."

"Remember to stick with the group," Mom called after her. "And don't stay out too late. And don't eat too much candy. And don't play any pranks that could get you in trouble."

4

"I know, I know," Emily called back. She was already halfway out the door. "Bye, Mom! See you in the morning! Happy Halloween!"

Emily stepped outside. Dusk was falling, but it wasn't quite dark yet. The youngest trick-or-treaters, itty-bitty ghosts, pumpkins, and princesses, were already getting started with their parents. Emily grinned when she saw them. This would be her first year trick-or-treating with her new friends—and *no* adults—and she couldn't wait!

Emily paused for a moment and stared down the street. *Walk to the corner, turn right, three houses down,* she thought. Though Emily had only lived in Riverdale for a few weeks, she was pretty sure she had memorized the route to her new friend Abby's house. But everything looked different in the evening. It was getting dark faster and faster, which made it hard to spot the familiar landmarks. Not to mention everyone who lived on Glenview Drive had done such an amazing job decorating their homes that they were almost unrecognizable. Gauzy cobwebs, flickering jack-o'-lanterns, and yards studded with fake tombstones were just the beginning. There were skeletons crawling out of the grass and a demon with glowing red eyes peering from behind a pine tree.

Emily almost felt like she was walking around the set of a spooky movie instead of her new neighborhood.

Soon enough, though, Emily saw the green shutters of Abby's house. Every window was blazing with light, and Abby's mother was already in full witch costume, stirring a cauldron that was brimming with candy. Abby's dog, Chester, barked at Emily in greeting.

"Something sweet, my dear?" Mrs. Miller cackled at Emily in a creaky, witchy voice. "I promise the candy's not poisoned—only the apples!"

Emily grinned as she reached down to grab a miniature chocolate bar. "Thanks, Mrs. Miller," she replied.

"I love your costume!" Mrs. Miller said. "An alien princess—how creative!"

Emily wanted to correct her—after all, she was an alien *queen*, not a princess—but she didn't want to be rude. So instead, she said, "I started working on it back in August. Halloween is my favorite holiday ever!"

"You're in good company, then," Mrs. Miller replied. "Every year our neighborhood goes all out."

"I can't wait!" Emily replied. "Is Abby inside?"

"Yes, and Leah's here too," Mrs. Miller said. "They're downstairs, putting on the finishing touches."

"Thanks again for the candy," Emily said before she stepped inside and walked over to the basement door. "Happy Halloween!" she called as she bounded down the stairs. "Hello?"

The basement was pitch-black, and no one answered Emily's call.

Weird, she thought with a little frown. *Maybe Abby and Leah are hanging out in Abby's room instead.*

Emily was just about to head back up the stairs when all of a sudden, a pair of hands reached out and yanked Emily into the basement! Emily screamed as she stumbled down the last step and landed on the floor.

That's when someone turned on the lights. Emily looked up to see Leah and Abby doubled over, giggling so hard they couldn't even stand upright.

"You guys!" Emily yelled—but she wasn't really mad. "I totally could've broken my ankle or something!"

"You screamed so loud!" Leah said, still laughing.

But Abby looked concerned. "I'm sorry, Em," she said, holding out her hand to help Emily get up. "Are you okay? We were just trying to play a good Halloween trick on you, but I guess it kind of backfired."

7

"I'm fine," Emily assured the other girls. "And it *was* a good trick. I was sure you guys were upstairs. You definitely got me!"

Emily looked around the basement. It was all set up for the sleepover that night with sleeping bags and pillows. Abby's mom's black cat, Eddie, lounged on one of the blankets.

"Your costume looks *amazing*," Abby gushed. "Alien queen! Too cool!"

Emily smiled and tossed her head so that her tentacle-hair glittered in the light. "You guys look great too. Leah, I have *never* seen a ghost cheerleader before. Where did you come up with that idea?"

"Well, just being a cheerleader didn't seem spooky enough," Leah replied. "But a vengeful ghost cheerleader who's not ready to accept her untimely death? Yeah, I could totally get behind that!"

Emily and Abby giggled. "How about you, Abby?" Emily asked. "Where'd you get your costume idea?"

"A little bit from Leah, and a little bit from my broken ankle last year," Abby replied. "Seeing the X-rays were so cool, so I was definitely thinking skeleton—"

"But just being a skeleton would be so totally generic,"

Leah interrupted her. "So I suggested skeleton ballerina instead."

"The coolest part is that the bones glow in the dark—and so does my tutu," Abby added. "Check it out!"

Leah turned the lights off, flooding the basement with darkness. Emily immediately appreciated the creepy effect as Abby struck a ballerina pose. The bones printed on her leotard and leggings gleamed with the same ghastly green as her tutu.

"Seriously creepy," Emily said approvingly as Leah turned the lights back on.

"Why, thank you," someone else said.

The girls turned to see their other close friend, Nora Lewis, descending the stairs.

"Ooh, vampire!" Abby said. "Looking good!"

"Nora's a total traditionalist," Leah whispered loudly to Emily. "And we love her for it!"

"Well, you can't go wrong with fangs," Nora said, grinning to reveal her new pointed teeth.

"All right, enough chitchat," Leah announced. "Who's ready to trick-or-treat?"

"Me!" the other girls yelled in unison.

"Did everybody bring a treat bag?" Abby asked. "I

have some extra pillowcases if you forgot one."

Leah started to laugh. "Forget my treat bag on Halloween?" she said. "That would be like forgetting my backpack on the first day of school!"

The girls thundered up the stairs. Mrs. Miller was still on the front porch, doing her best witch impression. "Take an apple!" she croaked.

"Ha-ha, Mom, very funny with the poisoned apples," Abby said.

"No, really. Take an apple," Mrs. Miller said in her regular voice. "I know how much candy you girls are going to eat. At least start off with something healthy, please!"

"Sure, Mom," Abby said with a sigh as she grabbed a bright red apple from the basket on the porch. Emily and the other girls took one too.

"Be home by nine o'clock," Mrs. Miller said. "And have fun!"

"Bye, Mrs. Miller!" Abby's friends chorused. Then they set off down the path.

"Where should we go first?" Nora asked.

"I have it all figured out," Abby replied. "We'll do Alpine Lane first. There's a house that gives out full-size candy bars, but they run out early so we don't want to miss it. Then Poplar Street, Ivy Lane, and Thistledown Drive."

"Hey, you forgot Hemlock Street," Leah spoke up.

"No I didn't," Abby replied. "I was just saving the best for last!"

"What's so special about Hemlock Street?" asked Emily. She walked down Hemlock every day to get to school, past the grassy lawns and ordinary-looking houses.

"The Randolph house!" Abby, Leah, and Nora said, all at the same time. Then they dissolved into giggles.

Emily raised her eyebrows. "I'm listening."

"They are *legendary*," Abby gushed. "Every year, they decorate their entire house with a different scary theme. It's too bad Chloe's family moved away this summer before she could experience one more Halloween visiting the Randolph house. It was always her favorite."

"I wouldn't even call it scary," Nora chimed in. "It's more like terrifying!"

"Oh, it's not that bad," Leah said, flicking her head so that her ponytail swung over her shoulder. "It's a fun haunted house, that's all."

"Bring it on!" Emily cheered. "When we lived in New York City, we would trick-or-treat in my apartment building. It was fine, you know, but kind of dull. Nobody ever did up their apartment like a haunted house. The most they would do is put this boring orange sign on the door so that you'd know they were giving out candy."

Abby's mouth dropped open. "Do you mean to tell me this is the first time you're going trick-or-treating for *real*?" she asked. "Like, outside, with decorations, and leaves on the ground, and dark night surrounding you?"

Emily nodded. "It is!" she exclaimed. "I have been counting down to this night for *ages*."

"Then what are we waiting for?" Abby asked. She linked her arm through Emily's and the two girls raced down the sidewalk, laughing so loudly that their voices echoed off the street.

The Randolph house must be truly epic if it's even better than this, Emily thought as she pushed her way through a maze of cobwebs just to get to the front door of their first house. It was easy to see why Halloween was such a big deal in Riverdale. The very air seemed haunted in the best way: a spooky chill that crept over everyone, making their eyes grow brighter and their hearts beat faster. And unlike the halfhearted attempts of Emily's neighbors in her old apartment building, it was clear that everyone in this neighborhood cared about Halloween as much as she did. There wasn't a single house without at least two flickering jack-o'-lanterns in front, and all the porch lights were blazing. Even some of the adults had dressed up, just like Abby's mom. There was one man dressed up like a pirate, handing out candy from a glowing treasure chest!

Emily was having so much fun that the minutes slipped away faster than ever. Her treat bag grew heavier and heavier until it was bulging with candy. "Check this out!" she crowed, hoisting her bag up with both hands. "I've never had a candy haul like this!"

"We pretty much covered the entire neighborhood," Leah agreed as she glanced into her own treat bag. "Not bad!"

"You know what that means . . ." Nora said with a sly smile.

Emily's heartbeat quickened. "The Randolph house? Already?" she asked.

"Well, it *is* almost nine o'clock," Abby pointed out. "My mom won't be happy if we stay out much later."

"I'm just surprised by how late it is," Emily replied. "Though I guess I shouldn't be. If I put much more candy in my treat bag, it will probably burst at the seams! So where is the Randolph house, anyway?"

Nora pointed down to the end of the street. "Last house before the nature preserve," she added. "I think that's one of the things that makes it so spooky. It's really quiet down there . . . even at peak trick-or-treat."

"Plus, the little kids are too scared to go there," added Leah. "But we're not . . . right?"

"Right!" the girls chorused.

"So let's go!" Abby announced, leading everyone in the direction of the Randolph house. Emily might have been surprised by how late it was a few minutes ago, but as she walked down the sidewalk, she noticed that several houses had started turning off their porch lights. She felt a sudden pang of sadness. Trick-or-treating was almost over for another year—and so far, it had been the best Halloween ever.

Emily tried to shake off the gloomy feeling. After all, it was early in the evening. There was still the spooky Randolph house, and of course the sleepover at Abby's was yet to come. Trick-or-treating might be ending, but Halloween night had barely begun!

"We're here," Nora whispered suddenly, jolting Emily out of her thoughts. Behind a wrought iron gate, the Randolph house loomed ominously. It was three stories tall, with balconies and . . . Emily tilted her head in confusion . . . *bars* on the windows?

"What's up with the bars?" she asked.

Abby shrugged. "I think they're part of the decorations," she replied. "I don't remember them from last year."

"Oh. Got it," Emily replied.

Abby nudged Emily forward. "Last house of the night," she said. "You want it?"

"Really?" Emily asked, glancing around at her other friends to see if it was okay with them, too. Emily was the new kid. Somehow, it didn't seem right for her to ring the doorbell at the Randolph house, the one trick-or-treat stop that everyone had been talking about all night. But Nora and Leah nodded enthusiastically.

"Yes! You do it," Leah urged her. "If you dare!"

"Ha-ha," Emily said, just to show her friends she wasn't scared. And she wasn't—not really. Emily had been to haunted houses before. She knew that they were all pretend, like a play or a movie set. Her hand wasn't even shaking as she reached out and pushed hard on the doorbell.

Ding-dong!

Emily took a small half step back and waited expectantly for someone to answer the door. *Witches?* she wondered. *Ghosts? Maybe vampires?* The outside of the Randolph house was pretty creepy, but it didn't offer any clues about what would be waiting inside.

The seconds slipped away while the girls waited, more and more impatiently, for the door to open.

"Do you think we're too late?" Emily finally asked. "Maybe they've shut down for the night."

"No way," Leah replied. "Not the Randolph house. Go ahead, ring it again."

"Okay," Emily said with a shrug. Her finger was just inches from the doorbell when the door suddenly swung open . . .

And someone grabbed her wrist!

Emily thought she would scream; she thought she would jump; she thought she would do anything but freeze. She stared straight ahead . . . stared at the gray, cold flesh that felt so clammy and uncomfortable against her own skin . . . stared at the festering wounds and crumbling scabs on the dead hand that was pulling her—no, *dragging her*—

Zombie, Emily thought as a terrible realization took hold of her. The heavy numbness left her arms and legs as her heart started thundering. She understood one thing and one thing only: She had to escape, *now, now, now!*

CHAPTER 2

Emily's treat bag slipped from her shaking fingers. As it fell onto the porch, dozens of pieces of candy exploded out of it. She felt the creature's grip loosen from the surprise. It was the perfect diversion; Emily wrenched her hand away and took off running—across the porch, down the steps, along the path, until she reached the sidewalk. And then she ran even faster, not even paying attention to the street names. She wasn't entirely sure where she was when she finally paused to catch her breath.

The trick-or-treaters had all gone home. The streets were almost completely deserted now, but the clouds had parted enough so that Emily could read the street signs by the light of the moon. She was standing at the corner of Evergreen and Poplar, wracking her brain about which direction would lead her back home, when she heard someone calling her name.

"Emily! Emily!"

"Wait!"

A hot wave of embarrassment washed over Emily as she recognized her friends' voices. What would her friends think of her now? She had never imagined she would panic like that at the Randolph house. But then again, she'd never imagined that they would have done a zombie theme. Zombie. Even thinking the word made her shudder. Emily's wrist tingled, as if she could still feel that cold, clammy hand grasping her skin . . .

"Emily! Hey! Are you okay?"

At the sound of Abby's voice, Emily braced herself for whatever expression might be on her friend's face. Would Abby start laughing at her? Or worse—regret befriending a giant baby?

But when Emily looked at Abby, she saw only concern.

"I—" Emily began.

"It's okay," Abby said. "You're safe."

Emily felt the back of her neck get hot. She forced herself to smile like everything was okay. "I know," she said. "It's just—I have a thing about zombies. Sorry for flipping out. That was so not cool."

"Please," Abby said. "It's fine. We were worried about you."

Just then Nora and Leah ran up to them. "Em! Are you okay?" Leah asked.

"Sorry," Emily repeated. "I really didn't mean to panic like that. I just hate zombies. Like, *hate* them."

"Well, obviously," Leah said, raising her eyebrows in a way that made everyone laugh—even Emily.

"I know you know this," Abby began, "but there's no such thing as zombies. I promise. You have nothing to worry about."

"I know," Emily replied, nodding in agreement. Rationally, she did know that. But there was something about zombies that chilled her to the core, filling her with intense and agonizing fear.

"Dead is dead," added Leah. "I mean, on the very face of it, the idea of zombies is ridiculous. People who can still get up and move? There's just no way."

"Thanks for trying to make me feel better," Emily

said. "I know you guys are right. Of course you are. It's just zombies have always scared me. And that one at the Randolph house . . ."

"What?" Nora asked as Emily's voice trailed off.

"Its hand was so . . ." Emily searched for the right words. "Dead-feeling."

She got even more flustered as her friends giggled. "I mean, it was like cold and damp and horrible," Emily tried to explain.

"We told you the Randolphs think of everything," Abby reminded her. "I bet that was why it took a couple minutes for them to answer the door."

"Yeah, Mrs. Randolph probably had her hand in a bowl of ice water," Leah suggested.

That made perfect sense—and made Emily feel even sillier. "Oh," she replied. "I didn't think of that."

"Trust us," Abby said firmly. "The Randolphs are pros. They spend, like, *months* planning for Halloween night. And they really do think of *everything*."

"I should've remembered that," Emily said sheepishly. "You did try to warn me."

"Em, is this yours?" Nora asked suddenly as she held out something silver and shiny.

"Oh! My tiara!" Emily exclaimed. "It must've fallen off while I ran down the street like a lunatic. I couldn't exactly be an alien queen without my tiara, could I?"

"Yeah, and if you were just a regular alien, then we *definitely* couldn't be friends with you anymore," Leah said. Emily joined in her laughter. After all, she was sure that Leah was just joking.

Pretty sure, anyway.

"We tried to save your candy, too," Nora spoke up. "Though if I'm being totally honest, I *may* have stolen one of your chocolate bars."

"I can't blame you," Emily joked. "Really, it's the least I can do."

"You're sure you're okay?" Abby said, looking intently at Emily.

"Positive," Emily said firmly.

Abby stared at Emily for a moment longer, as though she wasn't quite sure. Then she said, "Okay. Let's go back to my house. It's time to get this sleepover party started!"

To Emily's relief, she'd run in the direction of Abby's house; the girls were only about two blocks away. Mrs. Miller was just pulling her witch's cauldron through the front door as the girls approached.

"Right on time!" she called out with a wave. "Did you have fun?"

"We had an amazing time!" Abby replied.

"Probably the best Halloween ever," Leah added.

"Great!" Mrs. Miller said. "How about you, Emily? How was your first Halloween in Riverdale?"

Emily gave her friends a sidelong glance. "Let's just say I was scared silly," she joked—making everyone else laugh. It was easy to laugh now, with the lights shining so cheerfully from Abby's house, Chester wagging his tail in the doorway, and Mrs. Miller's warm smile beaming at the girls from the front steps. The Randolph house and that clammy hand seemed miles and miles away.

Emily followed her friends back down to the Millers' basement. "What do you want to do now?" Abby asked the other girls. "Game or movie?"

"Game, game, game, game!" Leah chanted.

"Okay, okay," Abby said, laughing as she held up her hands. "Game it is."

"Truth or dare?" Leah asked hopefully.

"Oh no," Abby said, shaking her head vehemently. "Absolutely not."

"Why not?" Emily asked curiously.

23

Abby and Leah exchanged a look. "Let's just say it's a long story," Abby finally replied. "I'll tell you another time. But I have a much better game for us to play tonight."

"What could be better than truth or dare?" Leah asked, sounding genuinely baffled.

"The spirit board!" Abby announced in a spooky voice. She reached under the coffee table and took out a battered-looking box. Emily could tell right away that it was old—*very* old. The wooden box was scarred with deep grooves and scratches; its hinges were tarnished; and Emily couldn't be quite sure, but it looked like one whole side of the box was blackened and scorched, as if someone had tried to burn it in a fire.

"Okay, I'm officially intrigued," Leah announced as she moved closer.

"The spirit board isn't just fun—it's spooky," Abby told her friends. "It's been in my family for a few generations. Apparently my great-great-grandfather made it, and it worked so well that he became afraid of it . . . and even tried to destroy it . . . but the board survived everything he tried, from being burned in a fire to chopped with an ax."

24

Nora raised one eyebrow in disbelief. "Really?" she asked.

"Who knows?" Abby said with a shrug. "It's a family legend. And, I mean, it certainly looks like the spirit board has seen better days."

"How do you play?" Leah asked, growing more eager by the minute.

It took Abby a moment to unhook the rusted clasp, but at last, she was able to open the box to reveal the spirit board. All the girls leaned closer as Abby eased the splintery lid off the box. Emily wasn't sure what was inside—but she couldn't wait to find out.

At first, though, the spirit board seemed supremely disappointing. It was a simple wooden board, not much thicker than a piece of plywood, with every letter of the alphabet burned onto its surface. The more interesting part, though, was a separate, flat, heart-shaped piece of wood with a small window cut out of it.

"What's that?" Emily asked.

"It's the planchette," Abby explained. "You put it on the board and everyone gently puts their hands on it—just your fingertips, not too much pressure—yes, that's it!"

"What is it?" Nora asked in confusion as the other girls rested their hands on the planchette.

"The way it works is that spirits can answer our questions by using our hands to move the planchette around—one letter at a time," Abby told her friends.

"You mean, we get possessed?" Emily asked. That didn't sound very fun to her.

"No, no, nothing like that," Abby assured her. "It's more like when our energy is on the planchette, the spirits can make it move. I think."

"But couldn't *we* just move it and pretend it was a spirit?" Leah asked. She pushed the planchette and sent it flying across the board.

"Well, yeah—but what would be the point?" asked Abby. "Besides, I would never do that."

"I wouldn't do that," Emily quickly chimed in.

"Neither would I," Nora added.

All the girls turned to Leah.

"Of course I wouldn't fake it," Leah said with an uncomfortable laugh. "Come on. You guys know me better than that."

"Plus, you can always tell when somebody's moving the planchette," Abby said wisely. "It feels completely different when a spirit moves it."

A chill of anticipation crawled over Emily's skin. She

inched closer to the spirit board, and the other girls did the same.

"So . . . what should we ask first?" Nora said.

A tiny smile flitted across Abby's face. "Can I go?" she asked.

"Do it!" Leah said.

Abby closed her eyes and took a deep breath. "Will Jake Chilson and I start officially going out soon?" she asked, in a voice barely louder than a whisper.

Leah started to squeal, but Abby put a fast stop to that.

"Seriously, *don't*," she whispered. "We don't want to scare away the spirits!"

Leah nodded without making another sound.

The four girls sat on the basement floor, the tips of their fingers just touching the planchette, for what felt like an eternity. Emily tried to focus, but after a couple minutes her mind started to wander. Everyone knew that Abby and Jake had been crushing on each other for a while now. Emily didn't exactly know what the holdup was . . . and she didn't feel like she knew Abby well enough to ask. She didn't blame Abby for wondering when she and Jake would officially be a couple, though.

Emily would've been tempted to ask the spirit board the same question if she liked anyone at Riverdale Middle School.

Then, without warning, the planchette began to move.

Emily tensed up immediately as it inched across the board. All the girls bent their heads close together as they peered through the window on the planchette, waiting for it to spell out an answer to Abby's question. But the planchette slid aimlessly across the board, never once spelling a recognizable word—or even pausing on a letter.

At last, Abby sighed. "Guess the spirits don't want to tell me," she finally said. "But the good news is . . . we're not alone! Who's next?"

"I have a question," Leah said. "Spirits, will I pass my spelling test on Monday . . . even if I don't study?"

That seemed like a quick and easy *no way!* to Emily, but she waited patiently with the others for the planchette to move. When it finally did, though, it still didn't offer any answers. The planchette's slow, uncertain circling of the board was not very informative.

"We must not be asking the right questions," Abby

said. "The spirits don't want to answer them."

"Want to watch a movie instead?" Leah asked, sounding bored.

"Wait—I have a question," Emily spoke up. "Spirits, what will I be when I grow up?"

The second the words were out of her mouth, the planchette lurched forward. Emily sat up a little straighter. Something had changed; the air in the room seemed charged, almost—and the planchette was zooming across the board with clear purpose, moving so quickly that it was hard at first to keep track of the letters it stopped on.

"Guys! Are you getting this?" Nora whispered.

"That was an *I*—" Abby said eagerly.

"And an *E*!" Emily added. *Movie star?* she wondered in excitement. But the planchette zipped right past the letter S to the letter Z.

"What's it trying to spell?" Leah asked, perplexed.

The planchette skidded over to O.

Then *M*.

Then *B*.

Then *I*.

And then *E*.

29

Z.

O.

M.

B.

I.

E.

"It spells 'zombie'!" Abby suddenly cried. The planchette ricocheted back to the letter Z, spelling the word "zombie" over and over again.

Emily yanked her hands off the planchette as if it had burned her fingers. Even without her hands on it, the planchette kept swinging between the letters Z-O-M-B-I-E.

"Stop!" Emily said, her voice higher than usual. "Stop it!"

The other girls pulled their hands away from the planchette too. It immediately stopped and stayed at rest on the board, almost is if it were waiting for the girls to resume the game.

"I can't believe you'd do that," Emily said, her eyes flashing with anger. "I *told* you guys I'm terrified of zombies. What, did you think that would be funny?"

"Emily, I swear, that was not us," Abby said right away. "I *promise* I would never do that."

"Me neither," Nora said.

"I wouldn't either," Leah assured her. "I like a good joke, but that would just be mean."

Emily didn't answer.

"Look, we saw how scared you were about Mrs. Randolph's zombie costume," Leah continued. "Making a joke of your fear wouldn't be funny. I promise, we're not like that. We're your friends."

"Then, how do you explain what just happened?" Emily finally asked.

"I can't," Abby said with a shrug. "Maybe it was our subconscious. Maybe we had zombies on the brain . . . no pun intended."

"But you all just said that you didn't make the planchette move," Emily said.

"We didn't—not on purpose, anyway," Abby said.

"Maybe our spirit is a prankster," Nora suggested. "And he—she—it—thought it would be funny? I don't know."

"And we probably never will," Abby said. "But Leah's right. And this game is dumb. It wasn't even answering our questions. Let's—"

Ding-dong! The doorbell rang.

CHAPTER 3

The girls froze.

"Is somebody else coming over?" Leah asked Abby.

Abby shook her head. "You guys are the only ones I invited," she said. Then she glanced at the clock. "It's nine forty-five. That's kind of late for trick-or-treaters."

"Unless they've come for the *trick* part," Nora said. "Abby! What if your whole yard has been TP'd or something?"

"You think?" Abby asked, her eyes wide.

"I have a better idea," Leah said loudly. "What if it's *Jake?*"

This time, not even Abby could stop the other girls from squealing.

"It is *so* not Jake," Abby said with a big sigh.

But Emily noticed that Abby jumped right up to see.

"I'm coming too!" Leah announced.

"Let's all go," Emily said. She was just as curious as the other girls—and she did *not* want to be left alone in the basement with the spirit board and its sinister planchette. She couldn't understand how it had spelled "zombie" again and again unless one of her new friends was behind it. She sized them up out of the corner of her eye, then shook her head. Emily just couldn't believe that any of them would be so cruel as to play such a mean prank on her. Not after the way she'd panicked at the Randolph house.

By then, the other girls had clambered up the stairs; Emily had to hurry to catch up. She found them clustered behind the front door, giggling loudly while Abby desperately tried to shush them.

"Stop!" Abby hissed. "If it *is* him—"

"Open the door! Open the door!" Leah cried, forgetting to whisper.

Ding-dong!

Abby's eyes lit up when the doorbell rang again. She didn't even bother to check the peephole before flinging the door open wide.

33

Emily could tell right away that the shadowy figure hunched on the doorstep wasn't Jake. It stared at her— her heart kicked like a frightened rabbit—with vacant, yellowed eyes. The grayish skin, the oozing wounds—

The zombie had come.

Had come for her.

Emily stumbled backward as she bolted for the basement, slamming the door loudly behind her. She sprinted down the steps and jumped into her sleeping bag. She didn't want to face whatever was up there. Whatever they had just let in.

Then the door at the top of the stairs creaked open. Emily stared up with wildness in her eyes. If it was the zombie—if he'd followed her—

But it was Abby. Just Abby. Emily tried to take a deep breath, but her lungs were too tight.

"Em!" Abby exclaimed as she hurried down the stairs with Nora and Leah right behind her. "It was just a late trick-or-treater. I promise, there's nothing to worry about."

"No," Emily said, shaking her head frantically. "You're wrong. I mean, what are the odds? First the Randolph house—then the spirit board—and now this?

They're *everywhere*, Abby, everywhere, and they're coming for me!"

Even as she said the words, Emily wished she could take them back. She meant every single one of them, though she could hear how, well, ridiculous it must sound to her friends. And sure enough, she saw the glances they exchanged. Her face grew hot with embarrassment.

"Emily," Abby began in a calm voice. Too calm.

"I'm sure you think I'm crazy," Emily said stiffly.

Abby shook her head. "No—not at all," she replied. "I think you're scared. Like, scared isn't even the word for it. Terrified, maybe. And whether or not zombies are real, your *fear* is totally real."

"It's kind of like a phobia," Nora spoke up.

"Maybe it is," Emily admitted.

"Why zombies, though?" Leah asked.

"I'm not entirely sure," Emily said. "I know I've been afraid of them for as long as I could remember. I think it might go back to this game my cousin used to bring over to my apartment when I was little, like in kindergarten. It was called Z Curse. She always said it was a one-of-a-kind game. I just thought it was horrible."

"I've never heard of it," Abby said.

"It was a board game with four die," Emily explained. "One had five sides, and the others had seven sides. Each side had a different letter of the alphabet. On every turn, you had to roll the die in hopes of getting a letter *Z, O, M, B, I,* or *E.* If you didn't get one of the letters, you couldn't move forward. And if you didn't get to the finish line first, you would be cursed—cursed to become a zombie!"

"That was a game?" Nora asked in disbelief. "It sounds terrible."

"So not fun," added Leah.

Emily shivered and rubbed her arms. "As you can imagine, I lost a lot when my cousin and I played Z Curse. I remember my cousin saying that zombies would come for me if I didn't win the game and they'd turn me into one of them," she said. "I guess it really stuck in my head. Because some part of me has been . . . waiting for zombies to knock on my front door for a long, long time."

Abby leaned over to give Emily a hug. "I promise you that's not going to happen," she said. "Not now. Not ever. It's just not possible, Em."

"I know," Emily replied. "On some level, I mean,

I know that. I know my cousin was just trying to freak me out when she described zombies—what they do, how they look, even how they *smell*—"

"Ew," Leah said, wrinkling her nose.

"You can imagine why I got so scared," Emily continued. "I was only five years old."

"I'm sorry, but your cousin sounds *awful*," Nora said with a frown. "So mean."

"Yeah, I guess it was kind of mean," Emily said. "To be honest, I think she had no idea how scared I really was. I tried so hard to hide it from her. From everyone. But when I see zombies—or even think about them—"

"Don't," Abby interrupted her. "Don't even think about them. Tonight's events were all just coincidences. Zombies are super popular right now. They're *everywhere*. Who knows why? A few years ago it was vampires. Who knows what will be next? Werewolves? Mummies?"

"Chocolate bars?" Nora spoke up.

Everyone turned to look at her in confusion.

"What?" Nora asked with a shrug. "Are you telling me that you wouldn't want chocolate bars to be everywhere?"

There was a pause, then everyone started laughing.

"Speaking of chocolate, who wants some candy?" Abby asked, shaking her treat bag. All the miniature candy bars inside rattled, their wrappers rustling.

"Ooh, me!" Nora replied.

"Me too," Emily said, managing a smile. She could see how her friends were trying to fix her night—make it more fun, more silly, more *normal*. And she appreciated it more than she could express.

Leah, though, didn't say anything. And that wasn't like her. Emily glanced over to see that Leah was focused on her phone, staring intently at the screen. "Earth to Leah," she joked, waving her alien-queen tentacle-hair in Leah's direction. "You ready for some candy?"

"Huh?" Leah asked, barely listening.

"Candy," Emily said louder. "Or maybe we can just eat yours?"

Even that wasn't enough to get Leah's attention. Emily's curiosity increased. "What's on your phone?" she asked, trying to get a glimpse of the screen.

At last, Leah looked up. "I did a search for that game you mentioned—the one you played with your cousin," she replied. "The Z Curse."

Emily's mouth was suddenly very dry. She tried to

swallow. "And?" she said in a raspy-sounding voice.

"Is this it?" Leah asked, shoving her phone toward Emily.

Emily's eyes locked onto the screen. She didn't want to look—

But she couldn't look away—

There it was, the Z Curse logo, as recognizable as the first time she'd seen it: a leering gray zombie head, topped with a golden crown, poking out of a massive heap of zombie bodies. It was familiar in all the wrong ways; just from looking at it, all the memories rushed back into Emily's mind. Sitting on the floor in her pajamas, playing with her cousin, wishing she could run away and hide under her bed—while Emily's mom and aunt and uncle laughed together in the other room, completely oblivious to what was going on.

"Yeah," Emily whispered. "That's it."

She was still staring at the screen when she realized that the logo was a little different, after all. It wasn't a photo of the board game Leah was trying to show her.

It was an app. The zombie head was moving back and forth, shaking its head like it was saying "*No, no, no*" with a sinister smile.

"Is that—" she began.

"Yeah." Leah answered Emily's question before she could even ask it. "It's an app now."

Nora and Abby came closer so they could see the screen too. "Creepy," Abby said. "No wonder it freaked you out so much when you were younger."

"It's kind of freaking me out right now," added Nora.

"Not me," Leah said. "It's kind of goofy, don't you think? I mean, look at the zombie's googly eyes! That's hilarious!"

"Are you kidding?" Emily asked, surprised. Sure, the zombie head had large, watery eyes, but they didn't seem silly or goofy to her at all. *How weird that two people can see the exact same thing—and interpret it totally differently,* she thought.

"I'm going to download it," Leah announced, her finger hovering over the screen. "It's free, after all. Plus, maybe playing it on a phone—with friends—will help you get over your fears."

"No!" Emily cried as she reached out and grabbed Leah's phone. Leah was so surprised that she didn't realize that Emily had taken her phone until it was too late.

"Give it back," Leah said, one hand on her hip, the other outstretched, palm up. "You don't just take someone's phone, Emily. No matter how upset you are."

But Emily stood firm, keeping Leah's phone just out of reach. "No," she said, and the strength in her voice surprised even Emily. "Not until you promise me that you'll *never* play that game. Or even download it."

"Oh, come on," Leah groaned. "It's just a stupid app!"

It was obvious to everyone, though, that Emily wasn't going to budge. "Promise," she repeated.

At last, Leah gave in. "Fine," she said with a heavy sigh. "I promise I won't download a stupid, harmless app that is honestly no big deal."

"Pinkie swear," Emily said, holding out her little finger.

Leah rolled her eyes, but she reached out and linked pinkies with Emily. "Anything else?" she asked.

"Yeah," Emily replied. "I want *everyone* to promise."

Nora and Abby exchanged a glance.

"Sure, whatever," Abby said with a shrug. "It doesn't really look like something I'd be into."

"Me neither," Nora added. "I'm more into photo apps and stuff like that."

"In that case, may I *please* have my phone back now?" Leah asked pointedly.

"Yes," Emily said as she gave Leah the phone. "Sorry about that. I just—I don't think that game can be trusted. Believe me, it's scarier than it looks."

"Sure, Em," Abby said brightly. "We believe you."

"And we've all promised not to play it," said Nora. "So you have nothing else to worry about."

Emily managed to return Nora's smile—but in her heart, she wasn't so sure.

CHAPTER 4

Emily usually didn't sleep well unless she was in her own bed—but in her whole life, she'd never slept so poorly as she did that Halloween night. With blackout curtains on all the windows, Abby's basement was exceptionally dark. Even though Emily knew, rationally, that there was absolutely no reason to be afraid of the dark, she couldn't help cowering in the face of its all-encompassing void. There was no telling who else might be lurking in that basement along with her friends. In the darkness, *anyone* could slip in unnoticed. It felt like hours that Emily lay motionless in her sleeping bag, listening to the deep, restful breathing of her sleeping friends. Emily didn't drift into an uneasy sleep until the gray light of dawn first appeared at the small windows, offering just enough light for Emily to assure herself that there wasn't anything—or *anyone*—in the basement who didn't belong there.

It felt like her heavy eyelids had just slammed shut when Emily was suddenly jolted awake. "Wh-what's wrong?" she stammered as she tried to sit up.

"Good morning!" Abby sang out from halfway down the basement steps. "Nothing's wrong, except there's only one waffle left, so if you want it, you'd better move pretty fast."

"Where is everybody?" Emily said as she glanced around; Leah and Nora's empty sleeping bags were piled on the floor in a heap.

"Upstairs, guarding the waffle," Abby said with a laugh. "Of course, I made them swear they wouldn't touch your breakfast."

"What time is it?" Emily asked, rubbing her eyes. She was still so tired; her whole body ached from lying on the hard basement floor.

"Almost ten," Abby replied. "You slept really late."

"I feel like I didn't sleep at all," Emily replied. She tried to stifle a yawn, but it was so big that it made her jaw crack. Then Emily's brain processed Abby's words, and her eyes opened a little brighter. "Did you say ten a.m.?" she asked.

When Abby nodded, Emily scrambled out of her sleeping bag. "Oh man, my mom's going to be here any minute," she groaned. "She promised to pick me up right after her yoga class."

"I'm sure my mom can give you a ride home this afternoon if you want to stay longer," Abby offered.

"Actually . . . I'd better get home," Emily said. The truth was that she couldn't wait to curl up in her own bed in her bright, sunny bedroom. She scanned Abby's basement and started packing up all the pieces of her alien queen costume. There was just one thing missing—her tiara.

"Hey, Abby?" Emily said. "Have you seen my tiara?"

"Nope," Abby replied. "Not since last night, anyway."

"That's weird," Emily said. "I thought I left it on the end table. But I don't see it anywhere."

"I'll text you as soon as it turns up," Abby promised.

Just then the door at the top of the stairs creaked open. "Emily? Your mom's here!" Nora called.

"Can I have your waffle?" Leah's voice drifted down the stairs.

45

"Sure," Emily yelled back. Then she turned to Abby and gave her a hug. "Sorry I was so weird last night. I hope I didn't ruin your Halloween party."

"Of course not," Abby assured her. "Besides, having someone who was legit terrified only made it more authentic!"

Emily grinned. *Abby is so awesome,* she thought as she started up the stairs. Emily still couldn't believe how lucky she was to have made such an amazing friend right after moving to Riverdale.

"Greetings, Alien Queen!" Mom said as Emily climbed into the car. "How was your hostile take-over?"

"It was fine," Emily replied, yawning again. "I can't wait to shower, though. I *maybe* used too much gunk on my hair last night."

Emily's mom was not the I-told-you-so type, but she nodded knowingly. "I just have to stop by the grocery store, and then we'll go right home."

Emily wrinkled up her nose. "Seriously?" she groaned. "You're going to make me go out in public like *this*?" Her hair was still filled with the glitter spray, but after sleeping on it, it was now sticking up every which way. She looked like a complete mess.

"Well, you went out in public like that last night and didn't seem to mind," Mom pointed out, the hint of a smile on her face.

"That was different. That was *Halloween*," Emily argued. "This is just pathetic."

"I only have to get a couple things," Mom promised. "It will be a quick trip. In and out."

Emily had no choice but to follow her mom into the grocery store. She stared straight ahead and pretended that she didn't notice all the people who did a double take at her spooky, sparkly hair.

"I think everyone's staring at me," Emily whispered to her mom.

"Only because you look so cool!" her mother replied. "Maybe you're about to start a new fashion trend!"

"Yeah, right." Emily sighed.

"Here, let's split the list in two," Mom suggested as she tore it in half. "Then we'll get done in half the time."

"Fine," Emily said. The first item on her list was cereal. She wandered over to the cereal aisle and tried to decide which one to get. She liked the granola that had chocolate-covered cherries in it. But there was something not quite right about the cereal boxes.

47

BRAIN FLAKES

ALL BRAIN

100% WHOLE BRAIN

Emily blinked and rubbed her eyes. She was so tired that for a moment, the letters seemed all wobbly. Then she realized that the cereal boxes read "bran"—not "brain."

Stupid, she told herself. *Of course the cereal isn't made from brains. This isn't a zombie grocery!*

Emily grabbed a box of cereal—she didn't even care which one anymore—and checked the next item on her list. Pork chops. That meant the meat department.

There were only a couple people waiting to be helped. Emily took a numbered ticket and waited for her turn, trying not to look too closely at the bloody steaks and glistening chicken breasts. Then, out of the corner of her eye, she saw something so disgusting that her empty stomach lurched: a mound of coiled-up flesh, the palest of pinks, glistening under the fluorescent lights. It almost appeared to quiver, pulsing in time to every footstep that passed. A sick feeling settled in the back of Emily's throat. Why was the supermarket suddenly selling *brains?*

And—by now Emily's stomach was churning, and she could barely swallow—why was the brain *pulsing* like that? It sat there, disembodied, shivering like it was still alive. How—and *why*?

Against her better instincts, Emily found herself creeping closer to the lump of brain. There was a glass case separating them, after all. She had nothing to be afraid of.

Right?

Closer. Closer. Closer. Until Emily's face was mere inches from the brain. It was even grosser up close—she could see flecks of blood—

And the tag.

SPECIAL

GROUND CHICKEN

0.99/LB

The laugh escaped Emily's throat before she could catch herself; once more, people turned to look. This time, Emily couldn't blame them. If she were trying to buy groceries and somebody with sparkling tentacle-hair started laughing, she'd probably stare too.

I have got to get out of here, Emily thought. *And I've got to get a hold of myself.*

Emily was seeing brains everywhere. If she wasn't careful, Emily worried, this zombie phobia was going to take over her whole life.

And Emily was not about to let that happen.

By Monday morning, Emily felt 100 percent better. She was ready to tackle the school day—even though there were still some stubborn bits of silver in hair. She'd spent the weekend hanging out with her family, with no cell phone, no TV, and lots of naps. As she walked to school, the bright November sunshine didn't just chase away the early-morning chill. It also seemed to chase away her fears. The terror of Halloween night seemed almost silly now that the sun was shining and all the decorations had been packed away. A few stray candy-bar wrappers that had been left on the sidewalk were the only signs that Halloween had just happened. And even though Emily loved trick-or-treating and getting all dressed up, she was ready to say good-bye to Halloween for another year. *I bet the Randolph house will have a totally*

different theme next year, she thought hopefully. *Halloween will be even better.*

At lunchtime, Emily was eager to hang out with her friends and find out how they'd spent the rest of their weekends. She was scanning the cafeteria, searching for them, when she heard someone call her name.

"Hey, Em!" Abby's voice rang through the cafeteria. A smile crossed Emily's face when she noticed the empty chair next to Abby.

"Hey! Thanks for saving me a seat," Emily said as she sat down next to Abby and Nora. "Where's Leah? I haven't seen her all day."

"She's absent," Abby replied.

"Is she sick?" asked Emily. "She seemed fine on Saturday morning."

Abby shrugged. "I don't know. Maybe she ate too much candy this weekend and woke up with a stomachache," she said.

"Or a 'stomachache,'" Nora said with a wicked smile as she made air quotes. "Didn't she have a test this morning that she wasn't going to study for?"

Abby started laughing. "Oh right, I totally forgot about that!" she said. Then she turned to Emily.

"Speaking of vanishing acts . . . what were you up to this weekend? I texted you like a hundred times, but I never heard back."

"I was washing my hair," Emily joked. "I took at least ten showers and I *still* couldn't get all the silver gunk out of it. Seriously, though, I mostly just chilled, no phone. It was kind of nice."

"Really? I could never do that," Nora said, shaking her head. "My phone is practically attached to me."

"Yeah—we noticed," Abby replied.

"You and the rest of Riverdale Middle School," Emily said as she looked around. It wasn't unusual to see students texting during lunch, but Emily hadn't ever noticed quite so many kids glued to their phones. *Maybe that's why it's quieter in here than usual,* she thought. She wondered what had captivated everyone. Wild gossip about a singer? The trailer for the next blockbuster movie? A hilarious viral video?

"Be right back," Emily said to her friends as she stood up. She'd forgotten to put a napkin in her lunch that morning, and she did not want to spend the rest of the school day with chocolate smudges on her face.

Thwak!

Emily was halfway across the cafeteria when another student slammed right into her. It was Veronica Murphy, an eighth-grader Emily recognized from chorus.

"Oh! Whoa! Sorry!" Emily cried as she stumbled. She grabbed on to Veronica to steady herself as Veronica's phone clattered to the ground. "Here—let me get that for you—"

To Emily's surprise, Veronica didn't respond. With a twitching motion, she jerked away from Emily and walked, stiff-legged, away from the table.

Weirdness, Emily thought. Veronica wasn't, like, her *enemy* or anything. Was she mad at Emily because they'd accidentally bumped into each other? That didn't seem fair.

"Veronica! Hold up!" Emily called. "You forgot your phone!"

Not even that was enough to get Veronica's attention. She stumbled onward as if she couldn't even hear Emily.

What am I going to do with this? Emily wondered as she stared down at the phone in her hand. Suddenly, all the color drained from her face. She reached out and grabbed the edge of the table for extra support.

Two words were blinking on the screen, over and over and over again:

YOU LOSE!
YOU LOSE!
YOU LOSE!

And there was the gray zombie head, wobbling back and forth, *laughing*.

Veronica was playing Z Curse! Emily realized as a wave of horror washed over her. Her mind raced as she tried to figure out what had happened. Veronica was playing the app—she *lost*—and then she started shambling away from the cafeteria, glazed-eyed and unresponsive. Emily started shaking her head on instinct. It was all too awful to imagine.

It can't be real. It can't be real, she told herself. *It's just a coincidence. I mean, it's just an app! There's no way that it turned Veronica into——into——*

Emily couldn't even bear to think it.

She glanced around the cafeteria again. It seemed like even more kids were staring at their phones, their lunches uneaten, completely oblivious to everything that was happening around them. Or was she just imagining it?

"Leah," Emily whispered. She remembered how intrigued Leah had been by the Z Curse app on Friday night. How Leah's finger had hovered over the download button, poised to tap it.

And how reluctant Leah had been to promise that she would never do that.

A terrible feeling started to creep over Emily. The napkin forgotten, she returned to her table. "Abby," she said, trying—and failing—to mask the urgency in her voice. "Did you see what just happened?"

"No," Abby replied, glancing around. "What's wrong?"

Emily placed Veronica's phone on the table. "Veronica just, like, walked right into me—and she didn't even notice," she said in a rush. "She dropped her phone and just *left* it on the floor."

Abby's forehead furrowed. "That's weird," she said.

"I know!" Emily said. "And look at this! She was playing that *app* and lost—See?"

The other girls leaned forward to look at Veronica's phone.

"Are you suggesting that Veronica played the game

and it turned her into a zombie?" Nora asked, her voice filled with doubt.

"I—I—" Emily stammered. "I know it sounds ridiculous. But who would just abandon their phone on the cafeteria floor?"

"Where is Veronica now?" Abby asked, glancing around the room. "I don't see her anywhere."

"I have no idea," Emily replied. "She was just, like, *staggering* toward the doors."

"Maybe someone texted her with bad news," Nora suggested. "Something really upsetting. That would explain why she just dropped her phone and walked away."

"Maybe," Emily said. "I guess we could check her phone for texts." She started pressing the buttons, but the phone was frozen. It didn't respond to any commands as the zombie head laughed and laughed.

Abby reached over and pulled Emily's hands away from the phone. "I don't think that would be okay," she said. "Going through Veronica's phone would be a major violation of her privacy."

"Of course," Emily said quickly. "You're totally right. I don't know what I was thinking. Doesn't matter, anyway—the phone is totally frozen. But here's the thing, Abby. I'm getting kind of worried about Leah."

"What does Leah have to do with Veronica acting all weird?" Abby asked.

"I—I don't know, exactly," Emily admitted. "I'm just worried, I guess."

Abby reached into her pocket for her phone. "I'll text her right now," she promised. "You know Leah, she *lives* on her phone. I'm sure she'll text me right back, like always."

"Thanks, Abby," Emily said, feeling a little relieved. All it would take, she knew, was one text from Leah and she'd be able to put these worries out of her mind.

After Abby sent her text, the three friends waited expectantly for her phone to buzz with a response from Leah. And waited. And waited.

"Where is she?" Abby finally said. "It's never taken Leah this long to text me back."

"Maybe she's asleep," Nora suggested. "I mean, if she really *is* sick, she could be taking a nap."

"Maybe," Abby said—but Emily could tell from her voice that she doubted it. "You know what? I think I'll stop by Leah's house after school to see how she's doing.

I could bring her homework so she doesn't fall behind."

"Great idea," Emily said, with more than a little relief.

"You guys want to come?" Abby asked.

"Sure," Emily replied. The sooner she knew what was really going on with Leah, the better.

But Nora shook her head. "I have my piano lesson right after school," she replied. "But text me after you see her. And tell her I said hi."

"You got it," Abby promised as the bell rang.

Emily glanced over at the clock. It was twelve thirty. There were still two and a half more hours until the school day ended.

How would she ever make it?

After school, Emily and Abby walked straight to Leah's house. They stood on the sidewalk while Abby sent Leah yet another text.

"Still no response?" Emily asked, for the tenth time.

Abby glanced at her phone again, even though she already knew the answer. "No," she said. "And I texted her again after sixth period. She hasn't replied to a single one."

Those words made Emily even more worried—and even more determined to find out what was going on with Leah. "We have to check on her," she said. "Look—the Rosens' cars aren't here. Leah's parents aren't even home. What if something's really wrong?"

"You're right," Abby said. "Let's go."

The girls didn't speak as they walked down the path that led to Leah's house. The door was painted red, with six faceted cut-glass panels in the front. Emily could see through the windows a little, but the carved glass was like a prism, distorting her view even as it cast small rainbows across the entryway floor.

There was a strange, eerie stillness about the house; it had an abandoned feeling, like no one was home. But even if Leah and her parents weren't home, what about their two dogs? Every other time Emily had hung out at Leah's house, the dogs were barking like crazy before she was even halfway to the door.

Not this time, though. This time, there was only silence.

"We should ring the doorbell," Abby said.

"You want to?" asked Emily.

"Not really," Abby admitted. "You?"

Emily shook her head. "Let's do it together, then," she replied. "One—two—*three*."

At the same time, Abby and Emily reached for the doorbell.

Ding-dong!

Silence. Silence. More silence.

"I guess nobody's home," Abby finally said.

"But what about the dogs?" Emily asked.

"Maybe the whole family went away?" Abby said. "And they took the dogs with them?"

But that didn't make sense, either. Leah told everybody *everything*. She wouldn't have been able to keep something like that a secret.

Emily stood on her tiptoes and leaned closer to one of the windows on the door. She pressed her face against the glass and tried to see into Leah's house. Everything appeared neat and tidy . . . and empty . . .

SLAM!

Without warning, the door shook like someone had thrown herself against it. Leah's face—her gray, scabbed face—pressed against the window. Her teeth gnashed, drool slid down her chin, and eyes were unfocused and—were they red?

Emily was frozen with fear. Too frozen to flinch; too frozen even to *move*—

She heard, as if from very far away, Abby screaming her name—

"Emily! *Run!*"

CHAPTER 5

Abby grabbed Emily's arm and pulled her backward. Together, the two girls stumbled down the path toward the sidewalk. Emily couldn't take her eyes off Leah's face, so empty, so *zombified*, as she slammed herself against the door again and again. What had happened to her friend?

But Emily didn't need to ask that question—not really. In her heart, she already knew the answer. Somehow, despite all Emily's warnings, despite her very best efforts, Leah had played the game—and lost.

Leah had become a zombie.

About a block away, the girls finally stopped running. Emily leaned against a tree as she tried to catch her breath. "Thank you," she panted. "For helping me escape. I froze up—I don't know why I couldn't move—"

"Forget that. What happened to *Leah*?" Abby cried. "Did you see her face—her *eyes*?"

"I know," Emily said, still shaking. "It was horrible."

"So she's just, like, a zombie now?" Abby continued. "She played that game and it really did transform her?"

"I—I guess so," Emily said. "I can't think of any other explana—*look out!*"

In the nick of time, Emily pulled Abby out of the way of another zombie who had crept up behind them so stealthily that neither girl had noticed. His arms were outstretched—his hands grasping at the air—

Emily and Abby both screamed, a high-pitched cry of pure terror. Then they ran three blocks to Abby's empty house (her parents were both still at work) and didn't stop until the door was firmly locked behind them.

"That was Wyatt!" Abby shrieked. "What—how—"

"It's the Z Curse," Emily said. "It's spreading—people download it, and tell their friends, and then *they* download it, and then they all lose. Every single one of them."

"And become zombies," Abby said. That's when

Emily realized, at last, that Abby believed her. Abby was on her side.

"If we could stop them from playing—stop them from downloading it—" Emily said, wracking her brain for a solution. "Maybe we should post about it or send a mass text or—"

Just then Abby gasped so loudly that Emily was startled into silence. Without another word, Abby whipped out her phone and started tapping the screen.

"What?" Emily asked urgently. "Abby, tell me. What is it?"

"Jake," Abby said with genuine fear in her eyes. "Last night, he texted me about this new app he'd downloaded—I didn't realize, Em, I didn't put it together, but he must have been talking about Z Curse!"

"You have to stop him from playing it," Emily cried. "Hurry, Abby!"

"I'm calling him now," Abby said, the phone to her ear. "Jake! Are you okay?"

Emily tugged on Abby's sleeve. "Put it on speaker," she said in a loud whisper.

Abby tapped the screen and held the phone out so she and Emily could both hear Jake.

"That app you mentioned last night," Abby began. "Was it called Z Curse?"

"Yeah," Jake said. "I haven't had a chance to play it yet, though. Max is obsessed. Leah told him about how awesome it is, and he's been hooked since he first tried it out."

Abby and Emily exchanged a look. *Now we know for sure what happened to Leah,* Emily thought—not that it made her feel any better.

"Was Max at school today?" Abby asked urgently.

"Only for the first couple periods," Jake's voice echoed from the phone. "He went home sick after study hall."

Emily shut her eyes. She could just picture Max Menendez playing Z Curse under his desk during study hall . . . and losing. . . .

"He was acting pretty weird," Jake continued. "I think he must've felt really sick. He couldn't even say much . . . he was just kind of grunting."

Emily didn't want to hear any more. She wandered across the living room and glanced out the window at Jake's house, which was right across the street. She could see him in the upstairs window, talking on the phone like it was no big deal. Like there wasn't a terrible danger surrounding them, growing closer every minute. . . .

"Jake, listen to me," Abby said. "Don't ever play that app. In fact, I want you to delete it right now."

Emily noticed someone shambling down the street. She recognized that swaying, unsteady walk right away; it was the same way Veronica had walked away from her in the cafeteria. But this wasn't Veronica.

It was Max—and he was heading for Jake's house! Emily was too far away.

"Abby," Emily said urgently as Max lumbered toward Jake's door.

"Don't even open the app—just delete it and then call me right back to tell me that it's gone," Abby was saying.

"Is it a virus?" Jake asked.

"Abby!" Emily cried, louder this time.

"What?" Abby asked.

"Look at Max!" she replied. "Tell Jake—warn him— tell him not to open the door!"

Abby nodded to show she understood. "Max is outside, but you cannot let him in," she said.

"What are you talking about?" Jake said. Emily could hear how confused he was over the phone. "He's my best friend; why wouldn't I let him in?"

"I'll explain later, but first you have to promise—"

Ding-dong.

Emily and Abby could hear Jake's doorbell ringing over the phone.

"I've gotta get the door. I'll call you right back," Jake said.

"No!"

"Wait!"

But it was too late.

The phone was dead. Jake had ended the call.

Abby ran across the room to join Emily at the window. "We have to stop him!" she shrieked.

"We can't," Emily replied. There was nothing the girls could do but watch in horror as Jake opened the door and ushered Max inside.

"We can't just stand here and let this happen!" Abby cried.

"What do you want to do, Abby?" Emily shot back. "Tell me what to do and I'll do it!"

"Let's go over there," Abby urged her. "I didn't even get a chance to warn Jake—not really—he has no idea—"

"Just hold on," Emily said, trying to think. "Maybe

he's not at risk. Maybe we're freaking out over nothing."

"Freaking out over nothing? Have you lost your mind?" Abby shot back. "You saw Leah trying to literally throw herself through a pane of glass to attack us. What do you think Max is going to do to Jake?"

"Maybe Leah was just trying to get out and she didn't remember how to open the door," Emily said. "But I was, like, right in Veronica's face in the cafeteria and she didn't do anything to me. If it really is the app that's caused all this, then I bet Max can't do anything to Jake. In fact, Jake will probably call you any second now to tell you how weird Max is acting. Then you can finish telling Jake everything."

A flicker of hope flashed through Abby's eyes. "You really think Jake is safe?" she asked.

"I don't know," Emily said honestly. "But I really hope he is."

An uneasy silence fell over the girls as they stood there, watching Jake's house, waiting for any sign of what might be happening inside.

"You want to call him?" Emily finally suggested. "Maybe Max isn't a zombie. Maybe they're just hanging out or whatever."

"I guess it can't hurt," Abby replied, reaching for her phone.

Just as she started to dial, though, Jake's front door opened a crack.

"Abby!" Emily cried. "Look—they're coming out—"

But the two boys who appeared on the doorstep were nothing like the fun-loving Jake and Max that Emily had gotten to know. From their vacant, red-rimmed eyes to their gray, sunken cheeks, the transformation in them was terrible—and immediately noticeable. Emily could tell right away that Max had turned Jake into a zombie!

CHAPTER 6

"I'm so sorry," she whispered. "I had no idea that the zombies have the power to turn others. Abby, please— say something—*anything*—"

Abby didn't seem capable of looking away from the window—or even responding. At last, she spoke.

"They're coming this way," Abby said. "Quick—make sure the doors and windows are locked. All of them!"

Emily rushed from window to window, checking each latch to make sure it was secure. Luckily, Abby's house was just one story . . . except for that basement. . . .

Emily couldn't bear the thought of going down there all by herself. Not now, when zombies were roaming the streets of Riverdale, and there was no telling what would happen next. She approached the door to the basement warily and noticed, for the first time, a chain lock near the top. Emily pumped her fist in triumph. She could secure the basement without even having to open the door!

"Everything's locked, Abby," she started to say as she returned to the living room. But Abby was totally engrossed in her phone. She didn't even seem to notice Emily's approach. The light from Abby's phone flickered unevenly over her face, giving it a grayish cast. And there was something . . . *off* about her eyes. . . .

"Abby!" Emily said sharply. "What are you doing?"

Abby glanced up; her pinprick pupils returned to their normal size. "I downloaded the app," she said.

"You *what*?" Emily shrieked. She lunged for Abby's phone, but Abby was too fast.

"Don't you see? It's the only way!" Abby argued. "We have to play it to figure out what it's doing to our friends. And if I can win—if I can beat this stupid app, once and for all, maybe we can save them! Isn't that what you want?"

"Of course it is," Emily snapped. "But you're just guessing that the app will give you clues. You don't even know if you can beat it! The stakes are too high!"

"They're too high not to try," Abby shot back. "I'd do anything for Jake. And Max and—and especially Leah. Anything!"

The fight suddenly drained out of Emily. She sat down and buried her head in her hands. "I know you would," she whispered. "I would too. I'm just worried. What if the app changes you into a zombie?"

Abby crossed the room and sat next to Emily on the couch. "I'm going to be extra careful," Abby promised as she put her arm around Emily's shoulders and gave her a quick squeeze. "If it looks like I'm getting close to losing, I'll turn my phone off. I'll destroy it if I have to."

The thought gave Emily a small, bright spark of hope. *The others didn't know what the app could do,* she realized. *But Abby does. And she can use that knowledge to protect herself.*

"Okay," Emily finally gave in. "I don't have any better ideas. Let's see what this app is really about."

"Let's do it," Abby agreed. She pulled out her phone and started tapping at the screen.

Emily didn't really want to watch—but she couldn't bear to look away. The app, she soon realized, was pretty different from the board game. It opened with a rotating maze—no, it was a map—and as it spun around, the path became clearer to Emily.

The words flashed across the screen in vibrating, bright red letters.

WE'RE WAITING FOR YOU!

"That's really creepy," Emily said. "Where do you think it leads?"

"I don't know—but you'd have to be an idiot to follow a map in some stupid app," Abby replied. "You couldn't *pay* me to go check it out."

"I wonder if that's where all those kids were headed," Emily said.

Abby jabbed her finger at the screen. "Enough with the stupid map," she said impatiently. "I want to get to the game already!"

As if on command, the map faded away, replaced by a whirling red-and-black circle. Emily blinked, and it was gone. A series of familiar yet terrible letters arranged themselves at the top of the screen: Z-O-M-B-I-E and then disappeared, leaving only spaces. The screen shifted again, this time showing Abby's ordinary, everyday living room—with one big exception.

There was a zombie sitting on the back of the couch, right behind them!

The girls screamed and leaped up. Emily spun around, her heart pounding—only to discover that there was no zombie after all. It was just a special effect in the app.

Abby burst out laughing. "For a second I believed it was real!" she babbled. "Didn't you? I mean, it seemed so real! I was convinced there was a zombie looming over us!"

Emily rubbed the back of her neck, which was tingling. "It was really just an effect, right?" she said. "But—is that the game? Virtual zombies sneak up on you and you have to—what?"

"Destroy them," Abby said confidently. "Like that loser over there!"

Emily snuck a peek at the screen and realized that another zombie was looming in the corner. With one quick motion, Abby swiped her finger across its neck. The zombie's head fell off. It rolled around the floor as the zombie collapsed, flickered, and disappeared.

"Yes!" Abby shrieked in triumph. "I did it! I killed a zombie!"

"Way to go!" Emily cheered.

A Z was added to the first letter space at the top of Abby's screen. Then that spinning red-and-black circle appeared again, for a moment longer this time.

"The app must be having trouble loading," Abby said. "Come on, come on, come on already!"

"Over there!" Emily cried, pointing. A new zombie was lumbering in from the kitchen.

"Pow!" Abby joked as she jabbed it with her finger. The zombie crumpled, flickered, and disappeared. The letter O was added, and then the red-and-black circle started spinning again.

"Just when I really get into this game, it has trouble loading," Abby complained. "I mean, what is this, the beta version or something?"

"Are you okay?" Emily asked all of a sudden.

Abby looked up from her phone and blinked. "Yeah. Why?"

"Your words . . . they sounded a little slurred," Emily said.

"No they didn't," Abby said. "I'm fine. Look! Another one!"

But Emily just couldn't get excited about the

app—not like Abby. A flood of nervous energy washed over her. She jumped up and started to pace as Abby began tapping at her phone screen again.

"Do you have to do that?" Abby asked without looking up from the screen.

"Do what?" asked Emily.

"Pace around the room. It's really distracting," Abby replied.

"Sorry. I'm just kind of nervous," Emily said.

Abby grimaced. "I'm sorry," she said quickly. "I forgot how much you hate zombies. This game must be torture for you."

"Well . . . maybe a little," Emily replied.

"I'll play in my room," Abby told her. "Just stay in the living room and chill. No need for you to worry about zombies. I'll come back in a few."

"You sure?" Emily asked, unable to hide the hope in her voice.

But Abby was already disappearing down the hall.

In some ways, it was better when Abby was gone. Emily didn't feel that creeping sense of doom that a zombie—even a virtual one—was lurking right behind her. But in other ways, it was much, much worse. She couldn't stop wondering how Abby was doing in the game; she couldn't stop worrying about Leah and Jake and Max and Veronica and who knows how many other unsuspecting kids from Riverdale Middle School.

Emily wandered over to the window. There were more zombies—a dozen, maybe two—wandering down the street. Even behind the closed front door, she could hear their zombified moaning and groaning. Their steps were somehow both aimless and purposeful; it was almost like they were on autopilot. Like they didn't know where they were going, but some part of them knew exactly how to get there.

Emily suddenly remembered the map in the game. Could they—

Then she shook her head. *They don't have their phones,* she reminded herself. *How can they follow a map they don't have access to anymore?*

Unless . . . she thought slowly, *unless they don't* need *their phones.*

Was such a thing even possible? Had the app, somehow, burned the information into their brains so that the zombie kids didn't even have to think about it?

"The red circle," Emily whispered. What if it wasn't a

signal that the game was having trouble loading?

What if it was *hypnotizing* the players?

Emily didn't know much about hypnosis, but she knew enough to piece together what might be happening. That spinning circle could be lulling the players into a zombie stupor, taking over their brains with mind control. Maybe it could even—Emily cringed at the thought—download information directly into their brains. The map, for example. What else? Is that what made it possible for zombies to turn other people into zombies?

If that's the case, the app won't need to exist for long, Emily fretted. *As soon as there are enough zombies, they'll be able to infect everyone else . . . until there's no one left.*

Emily was jolted out of her thoughts by the sound of footsteps behind her.

"Did you beat the game, Abby?" she asked, still staring out the window. "Listen to this—I just had the craziest thought—Abby? Is that you?"

There was no answer.

But the footsteps stopped.

In the silence, Emily could hear her heartbeat thundering in her ears. "Abby?" she repeated, her voice a hoarse whisper.

Still no answer.

Emily forced herself to muster all her courage and turn around. She sucked in her breath. It was Abby, all right—

Or maybe it *used* to be Abby—

Because the girl standing behind Emily had gray skin, peeling scabs, and pinprick pupils—with a spinning red circle glinting in each one!

CHAPTER 7

Abby lost, Emily thought. *Or maybe she never stood a chance of winning.*

But Emily didn't have time to dwell on that. Not now, and not with what she suspected the app could really do. She pushed past Abby—Zombie Abby was a little slow at first, almost like she was still unsure about how she had changed.

And in that regard, Emily surprised herself, too. That frozen fear, that total paralysis, vanished—just like that. Her heart was pumping hard, and all her muscles were tensed, ready to fight, ready to flee—ready to do whatever it took to survive.

Zombie Abby snapped to attention as she got ready

too. She lunged at Emily, but Emily was faster. Emily ducked away and raced into the kitchen, with Abby right behind her.

I have to get out of here, Emily thought frantically. But the front door wasn't safe—there was practically a parade of zombies marching down the street, and any one of them could catch her. Could transform her into—into—into one of *them.*

No, the back door was her only option. At this point, all Emily could do was hope that no zombies had stumbled into Abby's backyard. There was a forbidden shortcut through the nature preserve that would get Emily pretty close to her own house. Technically, Emily wasn't supposed to go into the nature preserve, but would anyone know if she did? If Emily could get into the nature preserve, she'd be home in less than a minute. And then she would be safe. . . . She hoped.

But first, Emily had to come up with a plan—and she had to protect herself. There was a small pantry next to the kitchen. She dashed into the pantry, slammed the doors, and locked them from the inside.

The windowless pantry was pitch-black with both doors closed. Emily reached overhead for the dangling chain and pulled it, filling the small room with light. It was very quiet in there, surrounded by boxes of cereal, bags of sugar, and stacks of canned goods. *I could hide in here,* Emily thought suddenly. *There's enough to eat to last for a long time.*

But just as quickly, Emily dismissed the thought. How could she stay hiding in the pantry with no clue about what was going on in the real world? She had to believe that there was still a chance to stop this before it got worse. And right now, Emily was certain she knew more about what was happening than anyone else.

Emily sighed, a long, jagged rush of air, as she paced back and forth in the small pantry. On the other side of the doors, she could hear Zombie Abby groaning and twisting the doorknobs. *Think. Think. Think,* Emily told herself, trying not to be distracted. Emily already knew how she would escape from Abby's house. She'd try to get out through the back door—she was pretty fast. If she ran as hard as she could, she could scale the fence, dash through the nature preserve, and be at her own house in no time.

But what about Abby?

Yes, Abby was a zombie now—but she was still Emily's friend. And she was utterly defenseless; there was nothing Abby could do to protect herself from the zombie hordes who were marching, marching, marching to—well, Emily didn't need to know exactly where they were going to have a very bad feeling about the situation. If the zombie kids somehow took Abby away, would Emily ever be able to find her again?

Abby has to stay in her house—for her own safety, Emily decided. If Emily could figure out what was really going on—if she could find a way to cure the zombie kids—

Not if, when, Emily vowed. *And when I do, I'll come back for Abby, and she'll be right here, safe and sound.*

But right *where?* Somewhere in the house, of course—but with all the windows on the first floor, it would be easy for the zombies to see Abby. It would even be easy for them to break a window and drag her out if they were determined enough.

Emily glanced around the pantry. Without windows, the zombies wouldn't know that Abby was there. But Emily wasn't sure that she could secure the pantry doors enough to prevent Abby from leaving . . . or zombies from getting in.

The basement! Emily suddenly thought. Why hadn't it occurred to her sooner? The basement was the most secure place she could think of. Abby would be safe there—as safe as she could possibly be with an army of zombies on the move right outside her front door.

Now all Emily had to do was figure out how to get Abby down to the basement. She needed a plan. She needed time.

If there was a way to lure Abby to the basement—to trick her into going downstairs, then locking the door behind her . . . Emily thought.

Then it hit her: She could be the lure.

Zombie Abby wants to make me like her, Emily said. *If I make her think that I'm going down to the basement . . .*

There were about a hundred things that could go wrong with Emily's plan.

But it was the best she could do.

First, though, Emily had to figure out how to get out of the pantry without Abby attacking her.

Emily tiptoed across the pantry floor and pressed her ear against the door. She could hear . . . nothing. It was strangely silent. She hadn't noticed that Abby must have given up on trying to get into the pantry.

But that didn't mean Abby wasn't waiting quietly just outside the door. Emily would just have to take a risk—and face the consequences either way.

Emily would face them prepared. She scoured the pantry shelves for something, *anything*, she could use to protect herself. If Emily chose the wrong door—if Zombie Abby lunged at her—

Well, the least Emily could do was be ready.

The only problem was that the pantry was not exactly set up for self-defense—let alone fighting zombies. The best Emily could do was a box of cereal in one hand and a can of soup in the other. It was so pathetic she almost laughed out loud—she could so clearly imagine cracking up with Abby over this—

Later, she promised herself. Emily needed to believe that there would be a time when this nightmare had faded to a distant memory, and she and Abby could laugh about it. Together.

Emily approached the door. Her shaking hand reached for the doorknob. She twisted it slowly, hoping it wouldn't squeak or creak or make any sound at all. Then, inch by inch, Emily eased open the door—

And stared straight into Abby's red-ringed eyes!

Quick as a flash, Emily averted her gaze. She knew that nothing good could come of making eye contact with Abby—not now. Not when her pupils were contracted to miniscule black dots in the middle of her unblinking eyes.

Abby let out a terrible sound, a choking sort of gurgle deep in her throat, as she lunged at Emily. But Emily was ready for her. She flung the box of cereal at Abby; hundreds of pieces of puffed rice flew through the air and pelted Abby in the face. Zombie Abby was caught off guard. She stumbled backward, swatting at her face as she doubled over. It was clear that she didn't even have enough brain function left to know what was going on. From the way Abby responded, Emily might as well have loosened a hive of angry bees at her.

It would've been heartbreaking to witness if Emily didn't have so many other worries pressing on her. She darted out of the pantry, pushing past Abby and running through the house until she reached the entrance to the basement. Emily paused for a moment, listening, then she opened the basement door and dropped the can of soup.

Thunk.

Thunk.

Thunk.

The can of soup rolled down the stairs, one step at a time. It sounded for all the world like someone descending the staircase.

Zombie Abby must've thought so too.

Emily could hear Abby's footsteps crunching over the puffed rice cereal as she approached. Emily braced herself, ready to bolt.

Steady, she told herself. *Steady.*

Then Zombie Abby turned the corner and spotted Emily. She immediately started moving faster—every fiber of Emily's body wanted to run, wanted to hide, but she forced herself to stand there, unmoving, unflinching, ready for whatever happened next.

Abby was just inches away—

Was reaching for her—

In one fast, sudden motion Emily ducked under Abby's outstretched arm. Abby was unable to grab Emily and instead kept moving down into the basement. On the top stair, Zombie Abby turned around, perhaps realizing that she had missed her target—but it was too late. Abby slammed the door shut.

And locked it.

A nervous laugh escaped Emily's lips; she could hardly believe it had worked! But the door was locked, she checked and double-checked just to make sure. Abby would be safe from the other zombies until Emily could come back for her.

Slam!

All of a sudden, the door shook. Zombie Abby, on the other side of it, seemed to have figured out what Emily had done. And it was clear she would try anything to escape.

Slam!

"I'm sorry, Abby," Emily called through the door. "I'll be back for you as soon as I can. I promise."

Slam!

Emily took that as her cue to get out of there—fast. She dashed through the house as Abby continued to throw herself against the basement door. A brief worry flickered through Emily's head. What if the door didn't hold? What if Abby was able to escape, after all?

The thought only made Emily run faster.

Before she burst into the backyard, though, Emily pressed her face against the window and scanned the area for zombies. She didn't see anyone outside. There was just a tall oak tree, its blazing crimson leaves fluttering in the wind before they drifted, one by one, to the ground.

How could it be such a beautiful day when the whole world was falling apart?

After another minute, Emily was convinced that the coast was clear. She shoved open the back door, stepped into the sunshine, and started to run. Fifty feet to the fence—

Forty feet—

Thirty—

"AHHHHHHHHHH!" Emily screamed suddenly.

She wasn't alone in the backyard after all.

Zombie Jake lunged at her from behind the oak tree!

"No!" Emily yelled, and the strength and power in her voice surprised even her. Zombie Jake paused, blinked—his pupils started to enlarge—

Then, like a yo-yo snapping back into place they contracted again, and he lunged for her once more.

But Emily was lucky. Emily's brain was still working, and able to coordinate all her muscles so that she could run and climb and escape, in that order. Soon she was over the fence. Soon she was racing down the abandoned path in the nature preserve. Soon she was climbing another fence, and soon she was in her house, with the heavy door bolted behind her. Then, at last, Emily was in her own room on the second floor, dragging her desk in front of it. It wasn't as secure as she would've liked.

But it was the best she could do.

Emily blinked as she looked around her room. It looked so ordinary, exactly the way she'd left it that morning. How was that even possible? The blankets were scrunched up on her unmade bed. Her pajamas were in a crumpled heap on the floor. And yet in just the span of a little more than a school day, everything— *everything*—had changed.

What am I going to do? Emily wondered. The words repeated through her mind, again and again.

Then she spotted the note cards—the ones from her half-finished history project. They were strewn across her desk, and though the history project was the last thing on Emily's mind, the note cards gave her a good idea.

Research, she thought, grimly determined. Wasn't

that what her history teacher, Mrs. Chu, always said? *It starts with research!* Emily would've laughed out loud if things hadn't felt so desperate. But maybe if she learned more about zombies—maybe if she learned more about this terrible app—then she could figure out how to fight back.

Emily flipped open her laptop and started scouring the Internet for information. To her surprise, all her searches for Z Curse turned up empty. *This makes no sense,* she thought. *I know the app exists. I've seen it!*

Was it possible that the entire Internet had been scrubbed? That there wasn't any evidence that the Z Curse app had ever existed? Her friends had all been able to find and download it.

So why couldn't Emily?

Unless . . . she thought slowly *. . . unless enough people have downloaded it that the creators took it down. They don't need the app to turn people into zombies anymore. There are enough zombies to do it.*

Emily immediately pushed the thought out of her mind. It was too terrible to dwell on, even for a second. She decided to do some research on zombies instead and clicked on the first link that appeared.

ZOMBIES: Real or Not?

The modern world's preoccupation with zombies, or the reanimation of the dead, is a relatively recent phenomenon. Many explanations have been proposed for the phenomenon, from contagious disease to hypnosis to sorcery. Experts agree that the zombie phenomenon is nothing more than a popular myth. But if that's the case, how can we explain why it endures—or how it began?

The fear inspired by zombies is very real. They lack the ability to reason or feel compassion. Reduced to their basest instincts, zombies are concerned with only one thing: creating more zombies. This can be done through a variety of methods, including scratching and biting. Theoretically, higher-level eye-to-eye hypnosis has the potential for creating more zombies as well.

Perhaps the least-well known—yet most intriguing—element of zombie legend is the story of their so-called king, Zyl. When a person becomes a zombie, it is widely accepted that the cognitive, or thought process, of the brain is destroyed, or at least severely incapacitated. However, when Zyl changed into a zombie, this did not occur. For reasons unknown, Zyl's brain functions at full capacity, even though his heart has not beat in centuries. It is this factor that makes him more dangerous than any other zombie in legend.

A memory flashed through Emily's mind: the opening sequence of the Z Curse app. That sneering zombie head, crowned with a golden ring.

Could the zombie king, with his unusual intellect, be the force behind Z Curse? And if so, who was he? And how could she stop him?

CHAPTER 8

Emily knew what she had to do.

She didn't want to do it—she *dreaded* doing it—and yet she knew, as surely as she knew anything at all, that it was the only way.

Emily stared at herself in the mirror over her dresser for a long, unblinking moment. Her unusually pale face, her hair, still speckled with silver spray—those were things she didn't even notice. It was the change in her eyes that grabbed her attention: They were steady, determined, ready for anything.

First, though, she had to figure out how to play the game. It seemed wrong to call Z Curse a game when it had become a matter of life or death—or perhaps *undeath*—but Emily didn't have time to dwell on the details. She couldn't download Z Curse onto her phone anymore; that much was obvious. There really was no trace of it on the Internet.

But that didn't mean Emily couldn't figure out a way to play it. All she had to do was find a phone that still had the app on it. But—and this was the most important part—Z Curse seemed to freeze the phone as soon as someone lost. Remembering Veronica's unresponsive phone, Emily realized that it was going to be a little trickier than she thought.

I need the phone of someone who downloaded the app, but never got a chance to actually play, Emily mused. *But who would that be?*

Surely someone in Riverdale hadn't played the app yet. But how could Emily find them?

One thing was obvious: She wasn't getting anywhere by pacing back and forth in her room. No, as much as it terrified her, it was clear to Emily that she had to get out there—out into the world, where the zombies were roaming freely—if her plan had any chance of success.

School, she thought suddenly with a flash of inspiration. There were so many clubs after school—Spanish club and band and cheerleading and drama and track and football. Abby looked at her phone. It felt like a lot of time had passed since she and Abby had left school, but it wasn't that late. There had to be tons of students still there. And, with all their extracurriculars, those kids probably hadn't even had a chance to play Z Curse—let alone lose.

Emily reached for her coat, shoved her phone in her pocket, and dragged the desk away from her door.

It was now or never.

She hurried down the stairs, peered through the peephole, and then cautiously stepped outside. The world was oddly quiet. Where were the cars driving down the street? The people walking their dogs? The kids playing in their yards while their moms watched from the front porch?

Emily shook her head and continued on toward Riverdale Middle School. There would be time later, she hoped, to figure out all the strange and puzzling things that were happening today. But not now.

Now, she was on a mission.

Emily ran the whole way to school. Powered by adrenaline, she didn't even feel out of breath when she arrived a few minutes later. The late buses had arrived and were idling by the curb, with billows of black smoke pouring out of their tailpipes. A strange, sinking feeling overcame Emily. It took her a minute to understand exactly why she felt so apprehensive.

Then she understood.

The late buses left at four o'clock every day—right on time.

And—she paused to check the time on her phone, though she really didn't need to—it was already 3:58. Where were the bus drivers, chatting on the sidewalk while they waited for the kids to clamber on board? Where were the lines of students pushing, shoving, and joking as they boarded the buses?

Where was *everyone*?

Run away, a small, strong voice inside Emily said, but she didn't listen.

She couldn't. Instead, Emily pressed forward.

The music room, she thought. Nora was the best junior pianist in the whole state, and she often took double lessons when an important recital or competition was coming up. Emily could only hope that today was one of those days. When Nora sat down at the piano, she was completely engrossed. It was entirely possible she was *still* playing, oblivious to the zombies that had been unleashed at Riverdale Middle School.

With wary steps, Emily approached the entrance. She could tell right away that her school had been the scene of something terrible. Lockers were half open, their doors hanging askew. The floor was littered with textbooks and pencils and loose sheets of paper that fluttered from the breeze that rushed into the hall when Emily opened the door. On the wall, someone had written RUN in large, red letters. The paint, still wet, was dripping onto the floor into a spreading pool.

It must have been pandemonium when lots of kids started playing Z Curse after school, Emily thought as she made her way down the hall. *Complete chaos. And total terror.*

But where were they? Where had they all gone?

There were abandoned backpacks scattered through the hall, so Emily did a fast search of each one, just in case somebody had left a cell phone. She wasn't surprised, though, when no phones turned up. She would have to keep searching.

Emily continued to creep through the hallways until she reached the music room. It was in even worse shape than the hallway. Stands and chairs had been over-turned; smashed violins littered the floor; and shredded sheet music was everywhere.

What happened here? she wondered.

Emily was painfully aware that the music room was deathly silent—but that didn't necessarily mean anything. The two practice rooms were sound-proofed. It was still entirely possible that Nora was practicing in one of them.

With one fearful glance behind her, Emily approached Practice Room 1. "Nora?" she called as loudly as she dared. "Are you in there?"

When no one answer, Emily knocked. Then she slowly opened the door. The hinges creaked so loudly that she jumped.

But the practice room was as deserted as the rest of the school appeared to be.

Emily approached Practice Room 2 next. She was feeling more and more discouraged. Whatever had happened at Riverdale Middle School, it seemed like no one was left to even tell her about it.

"Nora?" she called again. And then she opened the door.

At first glance, Practice Room 2 appeared empty too. There certainly wasn't anyone playing the piano. *Nora's long gone, like everyone else,* Emily thought. She'd have to come up with a new plan.

Then she noticed Nora's backpack was still on the chair.

And her phone was still on top of the piano.

"Yes!" Emily started to cheer—but the word was cut off, because two things happened at the same time.

Emily noticed the words—

YOU LOSE!
YOU LOSE!
YOU LOSE!

—were flashing on the screen.

And Nora lunged at her from under the piano!

Emily screamed, flailing her arms at gray-faced Nora. One of Emily's nails must have caught the side of Nora's face because a long, jagged scratch appeared on her cheek. It didn't bleed, though, and that was when Emily realized that if she didn't get out of there *immediately*, she'd be doomed too.

Emily darted out of the room, kicking the toppled music stands behind her in a desperate, last-ditch attempt to block Nora from following her. As she raced down the deserted hallways, Emily was grateful that everyone else was gone. The emptiness of Riverdale Middle School didn't just make her escape easier. It made it possible.

Emily didn't stop running until she was a few blocks away. Then, with her hands on her knees, she bent over to catch her breath. *Phone,* she thought. *I still have to get a phone. One with Z Curse already downloaded but not played.*

But how?

Emily racked her brain, searching for any possible option. Abby's phone was out. Veronica's phone, Leah's phone, Max's phone, Jake's phone—

Jake's phone.

Emily gasped. How had she missed it? Of course— Jake's phone! If Emily's suspicions were right and Max had actually turned Jake into a zombie, and if Jake had never even gotten the chance to play Z Curse, then his phone would have the app loaded and ready to go—and all Emily would have to do now is just play it.

Emily had to find Jake. And she had a funny feeling that wouldn't be hard to do.

The sun was still shining as Emily ran back home—no, not back home. To Abby's house. Because the last place Emily had seen Jake was in Abby's backyard.

Sure enough, Jake was still there. He was standing very still on the back stoop, his face pressed against the glass as he stared intently into Abby's house. *Does he know she's still inside?* Emily wondered. *Can he hear her banging against the basement door?*

Emily felt a pang of pity as she stood there watching Zombie Jake waiting, patiently, for Zombie Abby. He wouldn't abandon her, not for anything. Under ordinary circumstances, Emily could only imagine how thrilled Abby would've been to know, once and for all, that Jake really liked her.

But these circumstances were anything but ordinary.

Jake shifted a little, and Emily saw it—the glint of his phone as the sun reflected off it. It was shoved in his jacket pocket. For the first time that day, a thrill of hope spiraled inside her. Maybe she could sneak up behind him and slip it out of his pocket without him even noticing.

Maybe.

Emily crept forward, glancing down before every

step to make sure she wouldn't stomp on dried leaves or fallen sticks that would crunch underfoot. Most of the zombies she'd observed seemed really out of it—slow, thick-headed—but she didn't want to risk Jake hearing her. She'd seen how fast Zombie Abby was able to move toward Emily once she knew where she was.

Five steps to go.

Four.

Three.

Two.

Emily's hand was trembling slightly as she reached forward slowly, slowly, s-l-o-w-l-y, for Jake's phone. She had almost grasped it when—

Maybe Zombie Jake heard her after all.

Or maybe he just sensed her.

Either way, he turned around and stared at her with those red, fathomless eyes.

Emily locked eyes with him for half a second and saw . . .

Nothing. There was nothing there.

His eyes were like those of a corpse.

A tingling feeling started at her temples and crept toward her eyes.

She whipped her head back so fast that her neck ached. It was worth it, though, to escape the threat of hypnosis. Just because Zombie Jake's eyes looked dead didn't mean they were powerless.

Emily took a big step backward, watching Jake cautiously out of the corner of her eye. *Go back to Abby. Go back to Abby*, she urged him with her mind.

But it was no use. He'd noticed Emily now, and had forgotten—at least for the moment—about Abby.

As Jake stumbled toward her, Emily's mind raced. Every instinct told her to run away, but she refused. Not until she had his phone. But how could she get it now?

Only one idea came to mind.

Emily took a deep breath and ran toward Jake as fast as she could. He wasn't expecting it. Then Emily faked him out and started running in the opposite direction. Jake tried to turn as quickly as Emily had but he stumbled, and fell to the ground.

"I'm sorry," she said—and she meant it—as she darted forward and plucked the phone from his pocket.

Zombie Jake didn't move.

A cold fear overcame Emily. *Oh no,* she thought. *Is he hurt?*

Was it even possible to hurt a zombie?

Emily watched in silence, barely daring to breathe as Jake just lay there, motionless. She crept closer—Emily wasn't sure why—it's not like she could *do* anything, He was already a zombie—

But how could she just *leave* him there?

"Jake?" she said. "Are you—"

She didn't even have a chance to finish her sentence before Zombie Jake opened his eyes and reached for her. He was so fast that Emily didn't have time to jump back. His hands were tangled in her hair!

CHAPTER 9

Emily screamed and leaped backward. Her head hurt where strands of hair had been pulled out by the force of her leap. She caught a quick glance at Jake as he started to get up, her hair tangled in his cold fingers. Then she turned the other way and bolted through the yard, over the fence, and back to the safety of her own home. It was a small comfort to know that Zombie Jake was okay—as okay as possible, all things considered. It wasn't until Emily was inside again, with all the doors locked, that she felt like she could spare a moment to breathe.

Jake's phone was clutched in her hand so tightly that it had left marks on her fingers. Her whole hand was cramping. Emily rubbed it as she stared at the screen.

The app was right there, blinking, like it was taunting her. There wasn't a moment to lose.

Emily mustered all her courage as she tapped the screen. The phone vibrated in her hands as the app loaded.

Z CURSE
WE'RE WAITING FOR YOU!

The red letters on the screen seemed to glisten. Every once in a while, they would drip what looked like drops of blood. It made Emily's stomach clench, even though she knew it was just a digital graphic. *You're going to have to be tougher than that for what's coming next,* she scolded herself.

Emily tapped the screen. When the whirling red-and-black circle appeared, she was ready—and wise enough to look away.

The spiral dissolved, revealing Emily's ordinary living room—with the exception of a zombie lunging at her from the corner! With lightning-quick reflexes, Emily jabbed the screen, punching a hole in the virtual zombie's stomach. It collapsed, flickered, faded into nothingness.

Then the spiral was back for a second or two. Emily averted her eyes again.

When it cleared, Emily saw another virtual zombie perched over the fireplace. As it lunged through the air toward her, she smacked at the screen. It exploded into millions of tiny pieces, like zombie confetti. It was more satisfying to destroy these digital zombies than Emily ever could have anticipated.

Why have I been freaking out all day? Emily wondered. Those fears felt so distant now. Distant and impossible. Everything was going to be just fine.

The spiral appeared again. It spun slowly at first, then began to pick up speed. Emily watched passively as it spun. There was a flicker of a twitch at her temple, but she ignored it. Just like she'd ignore an annoying gnat buzzing around her face.

Everything was fine.

No.

It's not.

Emily tried to ignore it. But that small voice inside her was insistent.

It's not!

Something dripped onto the screen. It wasn't a digital effect this time.

It was saliva.

Emily dropped the phone and wiped her mouth. She was drooling—it was so gross, she was just sitting there *drooling* onto Jake's phone. And she'd barely even noticed.

"The spiral," she said out loud. Her voice was flat and empty of emotion, even though her pulse was racing. That's when Emily realized how close she'd been to losing everything. The Z Curse app was more clever than she ever could have dreamed. Slaying the virtual zombies was deceptively easy—and weirdly addicting. It lulled Emily into complacency—while the spiral twirled and twirled—

What's happening to me? Emily wondered, her mouth suddenly dry. Was it really that easy? A few fake zombies, the hypnotic spin of the spiral—

That rhythmic twitch in her temple—was it a symptom? It had happened before once when she had looked deep into Zombie Jake's eyes. *What was that?* Emily thought. *Maybe the twitch—the drool—that heavy feeling of calm—maybe they're signs that your brain is changing. And by the time you notice, it's too late to do anything about it—if you notice at all.*

Emily pulled herself off the couch and walked over

to a mirror. She stared at her reflection. She *looked* the same—didn't she? The whites of her eyes were perhaps a little more red than usual, streaked with vivid capillaries, but she'd slept poorly for the last few nights, so that wasn't cause for alarm.

Or was it?

Maybe Z Curse is impossible to win, she realized. *Maybe even when you're winning, you're losing.*

That, she realized, would be the cruelest trick of all.

On the floor, Jake's phone was still flashing. Emily didn't know what to do. She was sure, deep inside, that she'd had a very narrow miss. Who knew how close she'd been to slipping away forever—to losing herself to the zombie stupor that had already claimed so many of her friends?

Continuing to play the zombie-slaying game was not an option.

Which left Emily with only one choice: She would have to follow the map. Whatever that meant.

By barely glancing at the screen, Emily managed to exit the zombie-slaying game section without being further affected by the spinning dial. Back on the main screen, she breathed a sigh of relief—but only for a moment. The truth was that Emily was even less enthusiastic about seeing what trickery the map section had in store.

But what choice did she have?

Emily tried to psych herself up. *Twice they've tried to turn you into a zombie—and twice they've failed*, she thought. *You escaped from Max and Abby and Jake. You learned about the king of the zombies. You figured out the truth behind how the game turns you into a zombie.*

And now it's time for you to end the game.

The internal pep talk worked; Emily felt bolder immediately. She grabbed the phone and pressed her finger on the map.

Once again, the screen disappeared—and this time, it was replaced with an image of Emily's own living room, with a clear path toward the front door made of flashing red arrows. Emily blinked in surprise. *I didn't realize that the map would be augmented reality*, she thought as she glanced around the room.

Words, as red as blood, flashed across the screen.

YOU'VE HEARD ZYL'S CALL.
DON'T KEEP ZYL WAITING.
ZYL DOES NOT LIKE TO WAIT.

111

In the lower corner of the screen, an overview of the map appeared. It only took one glance for Emily to know where it would lead her: into the heart of the nature preserve. Sure enough, a small gold crown was blinking there.

Who is Zyl? she wondered. *Is he really the king of the zombies?*

Is he responsible for all this?

There was only one way to find out.

Emily pulled on her sweatshirt. The sun was hanging low in the sky; soon it would be dark.

Emily took a tentative step outside. On the front porch, she paused to glance around. There were still zombie kids staggering toward the nature preserve. She held up Jake's phone and looked at them through the app. To her surprise, their faces were wiped blank on the screen. No eyes, no mouths, no noses, no expressions. Just empty faces that made them look like plastic dolls. The sight disgusted Emily—and also made her more determined to win.

Maybe that's a sign! she thought suddenly. *If someone's face appears blank on the screen, maybe it confirms that they're a zombie.*

It was an interesting theory—but she had to test it out to be sure. Emily took a deep breath and hurried over to the car parked in her neighbor's driveway. She glanced at her reflection in the side mirror as she held up the phone. To her immense relief, her face on the screen still showed all her features intact.

Just then Emily heard the sound of her mom's car pulling into the driveway. *Mom's here,* she thought as an immense wave of relief washed over her.

"Mom!" Emily screamed. She ran across the yard, wanting nothing more than to throw her arms around her mother's neck. Mom would know what to do—it wouldn't be Emily's responsibility anymore, it wouldn't be her *fault.* After all, if she had never mentioned the game on Halloween night, no one in Riverdale would have ever heard of Z Curse.

Mom got out of the car and stared at Emily. Not smiling, not moving, not even blinking.

"Mom?" Emily asked in a small voice. "Mom? I need—"

Nothing.

Emily couldn't meet her mother's eyes. Couldn't bear it. With shaking hands she lifted Jake's phone and stared at her mother's image on the screen. Her face was empty, a blank canvas. No blue-gray eyes, the same color as Emily's; no crinkly laugh lines around her mouth.

Just nothing.

Emily stepped backward. Her mother stood there, staring at her. And that's when Emily knew for certain, knew beyond all shadow of a doubt, that her mother had become a zombie too. Because her mom would never have stood there so impassively while Emily was on the brink of tears. She never would've watched Emily suffer with that blank, uncaring expression on her face. In the last few months, Emily had been more annoyed with her mom than ever—doing everything she could to shrug away from her mother's hovering. In a flash of insight, Emily realized that her mom's hovering wasn't a sign of distrust or smothering. It was a sign of her love.

"I'm sorry," Emily said, almost choking on the words. "I'm sorry, Mom. I'll fix it. I—I promise."

Her mom just watched as Emily stumbled away. The only thing Emily could think to do now was follow the blinking arrows on the screen. Maybe it wasn't her fault—at least, not entirely—but wasn't she the one who had told Leah and the other girls about Z Curse? Would

Leah have even discovered that app if not for Emily? And now all her friends were falling like dominoes, one after another, as they succumbed to the zombie curse. Not just her friends, but her family—and so much faster than Emily could have ever anticipated.

What would it be like if Emily was the last non-zombie in the world?

Emily shoved the thought from her mind as she ran to the nature preserve, dodging zombies along the way. There were zombies she recognized from school and some she didn't. But they were all moving in the same direction. The same way she was going. She'd fight as hard as she had to—she'd fight as long as she could. Maybe today, maybe right now, she wasn't a leader or a follower.

Maybe she was a *fighter*.

And maybe that would make all the difference.

CHAPTER 10

Emily kept her head down as she stumbled through the streets, following the arrows back to the other end of the nature preserve. She remembered all too well what had happened when she had looked into Zombie Jake's eyes—and she didn't dare risk it happening again.

There was a rusty chain-link fence surrounding the nature preserve and Emily saw dozens of kids from school pressed up against it. It took Emily a minute to figure out what was going on. Then, with a sick feeling, she realized that none of them seemed to realize that all they had to do was climb the fence. Their zombie brains couldn't even figure out that much.

Strike one, she thought grimly with a shake of her

head. *Maybe you and your zombies are not so clever after all, Zyl.*

Either way, she was about to find out.

Moving stealthily so she wouldn't attract attention, Emily followed the chain-link fence until she reached an area where the zombie kids wouldn't be able to see her. The last thing she wanted to do was give them any ideas. Then she scaled the fence.

At the top of the fence, Emily took a deep breath and jumped. She landed on the ground with a solid *thud* that made her bones rattle, but apart from a scrape on her palm, no harm was done. Emily wiped her hand on her jeans and was almost grateful for the stinging abrasion. It reminded her that she was still human.

It reminded her that she was still alive.

Her heart reminded her of that too, as it hammered in her chest. Blood pounded through her veins and throbbed at her temples.

Emily checked her phone. The map seemed to lead her deeper into the woods. The nature preserve was off-limits to almost everyone. She wondered how long it had been since another human had stepped into its heart.

She wondered how long it would take the zombies to find a way in.

Warily, Emily paused to scan the area around her. There were no signs of other people, or other zombies, or even the wild animals that the nature preserve was meant to protect. She had never in her whole life felt so utterly and completely alone—not even on the very first day at Riverdale Middle School, when she didn't know a single person. Emily swallowed hard and tried not to imagine what life would be like if she wasn't able to stop Zyl.

How long would she be able to resist?

Forever, she vowed, even though Emily knew that might not be possible.

But to resist against Zyl for an hour, even for a minute, meant that she would need a plan. Emily rubbed her temples, which still felt kind of twitchy. Was it possible that Zombie Jake's stare—or the app—was still affecting her? *I'm fine,* she told herself firmly. *It's just the stress.*

She was *definitely* stressed.

But she couldn't afford to get distracted. She glanced at the screen again and saw that golden crown, flashing steadily. If her theory was right, and Z Curse was leading her directly to the zombie king, then she had to figure out a way to beat him—once and for all. Because

Emily already knew, deep inside, that she wouldn't get a do-over.

Think, she told herself. *Think.*

How could she defeat the zombie king?

Brute force was the first thought that came to mind—but Emily knew in her heart that she didn't have the stomach for it. Besides, it was a silly thought. What was she supposed to do, whack Zyl with a fallen branch? Pelt him with rocks?

No—her only option would be to outsmart him. She'd managed to find a way to trick Zombie Abby into the basement and lock her there. Surely there would be something Emily could do to outsmart Zyl.

If that article on the Internet was right, she mused, *he's stronger than all the other zombies, though. Smarter. There's that part of his brain that still works—the cognitive process, I think it was called. So that might make him even harder to outsmart.*

Then again—that might be the way to destroy him.

Emily stopped suddenly. If she was able to destroy Zyl's ability to think—if she was able to zombify the king of the zombies—

Would all the damage he'd done fall apart too?

Z Curse is rigged, she reminded herself. *No matter how*

you play, you're doomed to lose. But what if Zyl played? What if he lost at his own game?

That's when Emily realized that she would have to play the other game mode again. She'd have to risk it. But if he got close enough—and if she could give him a taste of his own medicine—

It didn't seem like a great plan. There were about a hundred things that could go wrong, and Emily wasn't even sure if her premise was right.

But it was the best she could come up with.

And she was determined to try.

Emily started walking again, following the path on the map. Her footsteps seemed deafening in the over-whelming silence of the woods. Why was the nature pre-serve so quiet? Not a single bird chirped; not a single squirrel chattered.

Did they know something that Emily didn't?

With her eyes glued to the screen, Emily crept for-ward. The trees grew thickly here. Emily had to push through their branches to move past them. If only she'd thought to bring a flashlight. Between the dense tangle of foliage and the fast-setting sun, it would be dark soon.

A message flashed onto the screen:

YOU'RE GETTING CLOSE.
ZYL IS PLEASED.
ZYL IS READY TO WELCOME YOU.

Oh, I bet he is, Emily thought as a flash of anger overcame her. She suddenly felt ready to confront him, ready to come face-to-face with the zombie king—and do whatever it took to destroy him.

Forgetting to be quiet, forgetting all about her plans for stealthy approaches and sneak attacks, Emily crashed through the underbrush and found herself, quite unexpectedly, in the center of a large clearing. Wisps of mist rose from the forest floor, as if from an underground hot spring; they snaked into the air, making it harder to see in the deepening gloom.

Something in the middle of the clearing glinted, a brief flash of light that startled Emily. She squinted as she tried to figure out what it was. It looked almost familiar—

My tiara, she suddenly realized. *From Halloween. What is it doing here?*

She stood in the center of the clearing, momentarily unsure, and then it clicked. That long, terrifying

Halloween night—she'd left it on the table in Abby's basement—but it had disappeared by morning. Emily had spent the entire night in a state of frozen fear, unable to shake the feeling that *someone* who didn't belong was in the basement. Now, though she didn't want to believe it, Emily couldn't deny the truth: The king of the zombies himself must have snuck in . . . and stolen her crown.

But *why*?

Emily didn't know, and she didn't want to find out. She glanced again at Jake's phone.

The gold crown was still blinking.

And then it started to move.

Emily's breath caught in her throat. If the app was to be trusted, Zyl was coming closer.

Coming for her.

Be brave, she told herself. *Be strong. Be ready.*

She tapped at the screen, adjusting the app's settings so that she could simultaneously keep an eye on the map—and Zyl's movements—while slaying virtual zombies. The split screen made it harder to concentrate; her eyes darted back and forth, back and forth, as she watched the crown approach while trying to destroy the false zombies that appeared on screen. *But it doesn't matter if I destroy them,* Emily suddenly realized. Zyl would always win some way or another unless she could face him directly. It was time to stop destroying the virtual zombies. Let Zyl think he'd won—and come to her.

Emily steeled herself. The next virtual zombie, she vowed, would survive. Even if the fear killed her.

Then she saw it. It was sauntering toward her on the screen, relaxed almost, like it somehow knew that Emily wasn't planning to fight back. She stole a brief, desperate glance upward to reassure herself that the zombie *wasn't* real; *wasn't* about to attack.

The clearing, mercifully, was still empty.

It will be over soon, Emily thought sickly as the virtual zombie inched closer toward her. It was almost right on top of her when, to her shock, Jake's phone vibrated loudly. The zombie grinned evilly as it vanished.

Did the spinning spiral last longer this time, or was it just Emily's imagination? It was hard to tell, especially since she had to keep her eyes closed to avoid its hypnotic effects. Emily had been afraid a lot during the last few days, but she'd never known fear so intense as she did in that forest with her eyes closed. Those seconds were agony for Emily. How could she monitor that golden crown with her eyes closed? What if, in those precious seconds, Zyl crept up—and transformed her before she even knew he was there?

Before the next virtual zombie appeared, Emily dared to glance behind her. She saw . . . no one.

Yet the golden crown was flashing on the screen. From the map, it appeared that Zyl was just a few feet away. *Where is he?* Emily wondered anxiously. It's not that she *wanted* to come face-to-face with a superzombie . . . but the anticipation, the waiting and wondering, was brutal.

How much longer can this go on? Emily asked herself.

There was a rustle in the brush behind her.

On the screen, the crown was very close. Emily watched it for several long minutes, but nothing happened. No movement. No noise.

It's like a game of chicken, she realized. *Which one of us will give in first?*

Then the crown started to move. It crept closer . . . closer . . . closer . . . until it was nearly touching Emily on the map. She swallowed hard. If the app was correct, Zyl was right behind her, standing close enough that she could practically feel his breath on her neck.

No.

Wait.

She *could.*

A wave of terror washed over Emily. It was so strong that for a moment her knees started to buckle. A frantic worry ricocheted through her brain—*will I fall, will I fall here, at his feet, on the ground, will this be the end of it, the end of everything*—

She locked her knees. Her legs stood firm. Even her fingers were steady as she swiped them across the screen.

Was she ready to come face-to-face with Zyl? No, not really. But would she ever really feel ready?

Probably not.

But Emily knew that she didn't have a choice. She sucked in her breath sharply as another virtual zombie approached. He was running for her—running right at her—

Jake's phone vibrated so hard that Emily's bones rattled.

YOU LOSE!
YOU LOSE!
YOU LOSE!

As the words spiraled on the screen, Emily spun around with her arm extended, phone held high. Zyl was there—right there behind her!

Time stopped.

Emily, horrified, couldn't look away.

There was no golden crown wrapped around Zyl's head, but a rusty circle of tin that left ugly gashes across his brow. His gray skin had peeled back from them, and it was clear from just a glance that each scrape was festering.

Zyl's mouth broke into an ugly smile that revealed yellow teeth and bone-white gums. The gray pallor of his skin—the sinister sneer on his scabbed, rotting face— the way his bony fingers were reaching out—

His eyes, though, were the most surprising of all. Unlike Zombie Leah, unlike Zombie Jake, unlike Zombie Abby, they were bright, glinting with intelligence. *Zyl really is still aware,* Emily thought.

Still, it seemed best not to stare into his eyes. Just in case.

Emily took a deep breath and thrust her phone at Zyl. He didn't understand at first what was happening. She recognized the exact moment when it dawned on him before the hypnotic spiral took effect. His eyes, reflecting the red spiral, flashed with panic. Then the light, and the spark, faded from them.

It was the perfect revenge.

CHAPTER 11

Emily watched in revulsion as Zyl's face went slack; a silver thread of drool slipped from the corner of his mouth. Then, as if in slow motion, his legs buckled beneath him and he collapsed to the ground in a heap.

Is he . . . dead? Emily wondered. Was such a thing even possible—to kill a zombie? Could the undead ever really die?

Did it matter?

Because in his current state, Zyl was no threat. He lay on the cold ground, motionless except for a twitching hand, his eyes vacant and unblinking. With the tip of her toe, Emily nudged his foot, then leaped back.

Nothing.

Zyl didn't even notice.

Emily couldn't smile—not yet. But for the first time, she let herself believe that maybe, just maybe, it had worked.

Maybe—just maybe—she had destroyed the zombie king.

There was always the chance that Zyl would snap out of his stupor. Or rise again, ready to convert even more people to his cursed, undead existence.

Either way, Emily wasn't going to wait around to find out. With one last look at Zyl, whose hand had stopped twitching, she started to back away. Then she was running through the deepening gloom, not even noticing as the tree branches sliced across her face, leaving thin, stinging scrapes on her cheeks. Her hopes were inflating like a bunch of balloons; Emily didn't want to get too excited—not yet, anyway—but for a moment she imagined what it would be like to return home and find that everything was back to normal. It would be a happily-ever-after better than any fairy tale ever told.

Wait and see, she tried to caution herself. *You have to wait and see.*

But a smile broke across her face all the same.

After Emily climbed over the fence, she realized that the crush of zombie kids had disappeared. Had they left earlier in hopes of finding a different way into the nature preserve?

Or was it possible that they'd transformed back into their normal selves, and wandered back to town on their own?

Oh, I hope, Emily thought as she started to run.

The streetlights were just starting to flicker on as Emily raced down the still-deserted sidewalks. There were so many people she wanted to check on—Max and Leah and Mom—but Emily already knew what she needed to do first. She'd go to Abby's house, of course; she had to free Abby, who was probably still trapped in the basement. Emily couldn't even hazard a guess as to what she'd find there. And in a few moments, she wouldn't have to guess.

She'd *know.*

Abby's parents hadn't come home; their house was dark and quiet. The banging on the basement door had ceased. For a brief moment, Emily wondered if Abby was still down there. Or if she'd fallen down the basement stairs—or accidentally hurt herself—

Emily shoved the unwelcome thoughts from her mind as she crept through the house with silent steps. It just felt wrong to be there, like she'd broken in, or barged in uninvited. She glanced over her shoulder warily, as though she expected someone to jump out and catch her.

But no one was there.

Emily approached the basement door and pressed her ear against it.

The silence was overpowering.

"Abby?" she called, hoping her voice was loud enough—if she was still down there—to hear it through the door. "Are you there?"

Emily waited for a response, barely daring to breathe in the stillness.

At last, it came.

"Em? Is that you?"

"Abby!" Emily cried.

"Can you open the door?" Abby's voice was muffled. "I'm locked inside!"

Emily unlocked the door. She flung it open, and there stood Abby, blinking, a little pale, a little confused.

But unmistakably Abby. Not Zombie Abby. Once

more, her eyes had that same bright sparkle that Emily remembered from before.

Emily threw her arms around Abby and crushed her in a giant hug. "You're okay! You're okay!" she babbled in relief.

"What happened?" Abby asked, still sounding dazed as she returned Emily's hug.

"You don't remember?" Emily replied.

Abby shook her head. "No . . . not really," she said. "There was something weird with Veronica at lunch. And you were worried that Leah was absent from school today. After that, it's just . . . blank."

"I don't know where to begin," Emily told her. "There's so much to tell you. The app . . . the Z Curse is—was—real."

A look of confusion crossed Abby's face.

"I know it's hard to believe. I know it doesn't make any sense," Emily continued quickly. "But—from what I can tell—it used a kind of hypnosis on the screen to shut down the cognitive part of your brain."

"My brain?" Abby asked in surprise.

"Your brain, Leah's brain, Jake's brain," Emily said. "And everyone else who tried to beat the game."

"You're telling me that I was a zombie?" Abby asked, still trying to understand.

"Practically everybody in Riverdale was," Emily explained. "The app wasn't just converting people into zombies. It was also leading them into the woods, where Zyl was waiting for them."

"Zyl?" Abby asked.

"The zombie king," Emily told her. "He wanted to create an army of zombies. And he was getting close, too." She shuddered involuntarily at the memory of all those zombie kids pressed against the nature preserve fence.

"Okay," Abby said. "So . . . how'd I end up locked in the basement?"

Emily gulped. "That was me," she said. "I'm so sorry, Abby. You were trying to beat the game but you lost and . . . you changed. I wanted you to be safe. . . ."

Emily's voice trailed off while she searched for the words. "So I lured you into the basement and—and—and trapped you there."

For a long moment, no one spoke.

"Let me get this straight," Abby said at last. "I turned into a zombie, and you locked me in the basement? For my own protection?"

"Yeah. That's pretty much exactly what happened," replied Emily. "Are you mad?"

"Mad?" Abby repeated. "Are you kidding? I'm *impressed*! Wow, Emily—I mean, I never would've guessed you could—wait, that sounds wrong. What I mean is . . ."

"What?" Emily asked.

"You were so terrified of zombies," Abby continued. "But look at what you did anyway, despite your fear. That was so brave, Em. You, like, saved us all. I don't even know how to thank you."

Emily tried to shrug it off. "Whatever. You don't have to thank me. I just did what I had to do, you know?"

Abby shook her head. "No way," she replied. "You've gotta give yourself more credit than that. I'm not sure I could've done all that, and I wasn't even that scared of zombies. Just—*wow*."

The doorbell rang then, and both girls froze.

"Oh!" Emily exclaimed as she glanced at the window. "It's okay, Abby. It's just Jake."

"Really?" Abby asked as she started fluffing out her hair. "Ahhh! I'm not ready to see Jake! I bet I look like an undead mess!"

Emily stifled a giggle. "You look *fine*," she replied. "Do you want to get the door, or should I?"

"I'll do it," Abby said as she jumped off the couch and hurried over to the door.

Emily moved over to sit on the chair. She hadn't told Abby yet about the way Jake had stayed in the backyard, waiting for her, unwilling to leave without her. There would be plenty of time for that later, after Jake went home.

"Hey, Abby," Jake said when she opened the door. A strange look crossed his face when he saw Emily—a brief flash of remembrance that was almost immediately replaced by confusion. "Did—what—" Jake's voice faltered as he tried to figure out what had happened.

"Are you okay?" Emily asked, instantly on alert.

"I have no idea what happened," Jake said. "My—my head kind of hurts. I think—I mean I can't remember anything that happened since this morning. It's like there's a big gap in my memory."

"Come sit down," Abby told him. "Emily will tell you everything. Trust me. It's a long story."

"I can't even find my phone," Jake continued. "Did I lose it? Did someone steal it? It's just, like, gone."

"Oh!" Emily exclaimed. "Don't worry, Jake. I have it."

Emily reached into her pocket and pulled out Jake's phone. The Z Curse app was still running, she noticed. She tapped at the screen, trying to close it . . .

And realized that Abby and Jake's faces were still blank on the screen.

They were still zombies.

No, Emily thought numbly. No.

They were acting normal—normal enough, anyway—but the app revealed the truth. Her friends were forever changed.

And they didn't even know it yet.

"What's wrong?" Jake asked.

"Yeah, you got really pale all of a sudden," Abby added. "Are you feeling okay?"

"Fine," Emily managed to say. "I'm fine." She handed Jake his phone. "I'm just going to—step outside—for a minute—to get some air—"

All Emily knew for certain in that moment was that she had to get away quickly. It was impossible to guess what could happen next. But Jake and Abby weren't back to normal—and now Emily knew that they never would be.

She forced herself to walk slowly, calmly, to the door. She'd get outside—away from Jake and Abby and whatever threat they posed. She'd go home—no, she couldn't go home—after all, Mom was a zombie now too—

But maybe the app is wrong, Emily told herself. *Maybe it's stuck on that setting with the blank faces. Maybe Abby and Jake are fine. Maybe I'm overreacting.*

Maybe.

But Emily still felt like she had to escape. And if she'd learned anything from this horrible waking nightmare, it was that she would always, always, always trust her instincts.

No matter what.

"Be right back!" Emily said in a fake-cheerful voice as she inched open the door. She pulled it closed behind her, hard, and heard the comforting *click* of the lock.

Then she looked out to the street.

Dozens—no—hundreds—no—*thousands* of zombies were approaching, their footsteps shuffling as they dragged their feet across the asphalt. And right in the middle, in front, leading them, was Zyl. He smiled at her with his cracked lips and Emily was sure she saw a glint of happiness in his red eyes. And that's when she knew that the past few minutes had all been a trick. Zyl was only pretending that Abby and Jake were back to normal. Zyl only pretended to have been destroyed by his own game.

A heavy weight of dread settled over Emily.

The zombie invasion hadn't just begun.

It was almost complete.

Zyl would be the king of all.

WANT MORE CREEPINESS?
Then you're in luck, because P. J. Night has some more scares for you and your friends!

ZYL'S MESSAGE FOR YOU

What message does Zyl have for you? Unscramble the letters in each of the words below and then write the circled words in order to discover his message.

PIRSIT __ __ __ __ __ __ (circle last letter)

ELHP __ __ __ __ (circle first two letters)

BMOZEI __ __ __ __ __ __ (circle first three letters)

INABRS __ __ __ __ __ __ (circle first and
    fourth letters)

SUOHE __ __ __ __ __ (circle last letter)

HOOCSL __ __ __ __ __ __ (circle first letter)

PPA __ __ __ (circle first letter)

SCUER __ __ __ __ __ (circle third and fifth letters)

MBNTEASE __ __ __ __ __ __ __ __ (circle first and
    fourth letters)

UAHNT __ __ __ __ __ (circle first letter)

GNIK __ __ __ __ (circle second and third letters)

CIDE __ __ __ __ (circle first letter)

UYO __ __ __ (circle all three letters)

MESTOCU __ __ __ __ __ __ __ (circle sixth letter)

RDOAB __ __ __ __ __ (circle third and fifth letters)

SERPEREV __ __ __ __ __ __ __ __ (circle last letter)

OUY __ __ __ (circle all three letters)

EEEEARRHLCD __ __ __ __ __ __ __ __ __ __ (circle sixth letter)

OYOPKS __ __ __ __ __ __ (circle third, fourth, and fifth letters)

__ __ __   __ __ __ __ __ __ __   __ __ __

__ __ __ __ __ __ __ __ __ __.   __ __ __ __

__ __ __   __ __ __ __!

Turn the page for the answer.

ANSWER KEY

SPIRIT

HELP

ZOMBIE

BRAINS

HOUSE

SCHOOL

APP

CURSE

BASEMENT

HAUNT

KING

DICE

YOU

COSTUME

BOARD

PRESERVE

YOU

CHEERLEADER

SPOOKY

YOU'RE INVITED TO . . .
CREATE YOUR OWN SCARY STORY!

Do you want to turn your sleepover into a creepover? Telling a spooky story is a great way to set the mood. P. J. Night has written a few sentences to get you started. Fill in the rest of the story and have fun scaring your friends.

You can also collaborate with your friends on this story by taking turns. Have everyone at your sleepover sit in a circle. Pick one person to start. She will add a sentence or two to the story, cover what she wrote with a piece of paper leaving only the last word or phrase visible, and then pass the story to the next girl. Once everyone has taken a turn, read the scary story you created together aloud!

Last night I had a horrible dream. I dreamed that everyone I know had turned into a zombie. They were all moving really slowly and moaning about brains. I tried to talk to them, but it was like they couldn't understand me, even my best friend. When I woke up, I was so happy it was only a dream. Until I went to school that day and saw . . .

_____

_____

_____

_____

_____

_____

_____

_____

_____

_____

_____

_____

_____

_____

_____

_____

_____

DO NOT FEAR—
WE HAVE ANOTHER CREEPY TALE FOR YOU!

TURN THE PAGE FOR A SNEAK PEEK AT

You're invited to a

CREEPOVER®

No Trick-or-Treating!

Click.

Ashley blinked in the sudden brightness. The bare lightbulb overhead swung from a rusty chain, casting shadows all over her new bedroom. She squinted in the harsh light, but it was the best she could do until she unpacked the little purple lamp that had sat on her bedside table for as long as she could remember.

Besides, she told herself, glancing from the boxes scattered over the pocked floor to the four-foot crack running down the wall, *it's not like this room could look any worse.*

Ashley sighed, for the thousandth time, as she remembered her old bedroom back in Atlanta. It was perfect in every way, from the pale-aqua paint on the walls to the window seat that overlooked the alley, a quiet place in a bustling city. But that was all gone now; Ashley knew she'd probably never see her room again. Maybe, right this very minute, somebody else was sitting in her old room, starting to unpack a bunch of boxes.

Lucky, Ashley thought, flopping back on her bare

mattress and staring at the stain-spotted ceiling. She knew she should put the sheets on her bed, but she just didn't feel like doing anything.

There was a knock at the door. Ashley could tell from the four strong raps that it was her mother. *Maybe if I ignore her, she'll go away,* Ashley thought.

The knock came again, and then the door creaked open.

"Hey, Pumpkin!" Mrs. McDowell called out in a cheerful voice. "How's it going in here? Want some help?"

The bed creaked as Mrs. McDowell sat behind Ashley and started rubbing her back. Ashley inched away. She knew she was probably hurting her mom's feelings, but it was hard to care. After all, it wasn't like her mom and dad had cared about *her* feelings when they'd decided to sell their apartment and buy this rundown farm out in the middle of nowhere.

"This is going to be a really great thing, Ashley," Mrs. McDowell said yet again. "Just try to have faith, okay? I know change is hard and stressful and scary—"

"Scary? Um, no. I'm not *scared.* I'm *bored.* I hate it here."

"You hate it here?" Mrs. McDowell said. "Pumpkin, we've only been in Heaton Corners for, oh, five hours or so. All I ask is that you give it a chance. You know Dad and I wouldn't make a decision this big if we didn't think it was the best thing for everyone."

"But you didn't even *ask* me," Ashley replied, blinking back tears. "I don't *want* to live on a smelly farm, Mom. I miss Atlanta so much."

Mrs. McDowell sighed. "We really regret not leaving the city before Maya went to college," she said in a quiet voice. "We don't want to make the same mistake with you. Maya spent her whole childhood cooped up in that apartment—"

"Yeah, and she loved it!" Ashley interrupted. "And so did I!"

"Can you try to think of it as an adventure?" Mrs. McDowell asked, and there was something so vulnerable in her voice that Ashley finally sat up and looked at her. "You know there's something really exciting about a fresh start, going to a whole new school and meeting all kinds of new people! And we'll have the homestead up and running before you know it—the chicks will arrive in a few days; won't that be fun? Little fluffy baby chickens? And next spring we'll get a cow!"

Ashley started to laugh. It was such a ridiculous

thing to say—"we'll get a cow!"—that she couldn't help herself. And she couldn't miss the relief that flooded her mom's eyes.

"And maybe," Ashley said, wishing that she wasn't giving in so easily but saying it anyway, "we can fix that horrible crack over there? It looks like the wall got struck by lightning."

Mrs. McDowell smiled as she patted Ashley's knee. "Of course. I'll have Dad come take a look—we can probably patch that crack by the end of the week. And then we'll get the walls primed for painting. Have you thought about what color you want? Maybe a nice, sunny yellow?"

"Aqua," Ashley said firmly. "Just like my old room."

"All right," Mrs. McDowell said. "Whatever you want. Listen, Dad went to get pizza; I think he'll be back in an hour or so."

"That long?" Ashley asked. "To grab pizza?"

"Well, it turns out there's no pizza place in Heaton Corners," Mrs. McDowell said, sighing. "So he had to drive all the way to Walthrop."

Mrs. McDowell stood up. On her way out, she paused by the door. "Oh, Ashley? Did I see your bike out back?"

"Yeah, probably."

"Go out and put it in the barn, okay?"

"Why?" Ashley argued. "We're in the middle of nowhere, remember? Nobody's going to steal it."

"Probably not," Mrs. McDowell replied. Then she pointed at the window. "But it looks like it's going to rain tonight. You see those thunderheads gathering? So go ahead and get your bike in the barn so it doesn't rust. Thanks, Pumpkin."

Ashley sighed heavily and went downstairs. Her flip-flops were near the back door, where she'd kicked them off after the movers had left. One look out the window told Ashley that she would need a flashlight to find the barn. Luckily, there was a flashlight hanging right next to the door. Ashley guessed that the last people who'd lived here had found themselves in the same situation.

She switched on the flashlight and stepped outside. Its bright-yellow beam pierced through the night sky, then quickly faded to a dull orange. Ashley shook the flashlight and smacked it against her palm until it glowed a little brighter.

Typical, she thought. *I bet the batteries will die as soon as I get into the barn.*

The thought made Ashley walk a little faster as she wheeled her bike through the overgrown goldenrod toward the barn. It hadn't started raining yet, but the weeds were damp with evening dew, and she shivered as they slapped against her bare legs. And her toes were *freezing*. Ashley hated to admit it, but her mom was right: Sandal season was *definitely* over.

Just before Ashley reached the barn, the flashlight died, but in a stroke of luck the clouds parted for a moment, letting through enough moonlight that she could lift the heavy iron latch on the barn door. The only sound Ashley could hear was the soft *squeeeeeeak* of the bike's gears as she pushed it into the barn.

The air in the barn was dry and dusty; it smelled of caked dirt and hay. The moment Ashley stepped in from the barn door, it slammed shut with such a loud bang that she jumped. Without even the weak beam of the flashlight to guide her steps, Ashley was plunged into pitch-black darkness. She stretched her arm out as far as it would reach, until her fingers grazed the rough, unfinished wood of the barn wall. Then she took one careful step at a time until she found a spot to leave her bike. Ashley leaned it against the wall and turned to leave.

C-r-r-r-r-unch.

She froze.

What, Ashley thought as her heart started to pound, *did I just step on?*

There was something leathery, something papery, something scaly, something she couldn't quite place—flicking against her bare skin. Was it slithering over her feet, twining around her ankles? Or was that just her imagination?

Had it been *waiting* for someone to set foot inside this old, abandoned barn?

Stop it, Ashley told herself firmly. She was a city girl. She was not the kind of person who freaked out over every little thing. With a surge of confidence, she hit the flashlight against her palm again.

Thwak. Thwak. Thwak.

Suddenly a pale beam flashed across the barn. The flashlight was working again, for a minute, at least.

Ashley pointed the flashlight at her feet. It took a moment—longer, probably—for her to realize what she was standing in; some part of her brain couldn't, *wouldn't* accept it. There were so many that she couldn't count them, especially because of the way they wriggled—

Wait. *Were* they moving? Or was that just the effect of her clumsy feet as she stumbled, trying to escape?

Either way, Ashley didn't stick around to find out. She screamed—she couldn't help it—as the weak light from the flashlight died again. Ashley rushed out of the barn, still screaming, and her screams echoed across the farm, almost as if they were ricocheting off the heavy clouds that were crowding the sky once more.

She was so preoccupied by the memory of those slithery *things* on her feet, and so distracted by the utter darkness, that she didn't see the tall figure step out from the shadows . . .

Until a pair of strong hands grabbed her shoulders and held on tight!

A lifelong night owl, **P. J. NIGHT** often works furiously into the wee hours of the morning, writing down spooky tales and dreaming up new stories of the supernatural and otherworldly. Although P. J.'s whereabouts are unknown at this time, we suspect the author lives in a drafty, old mansion where the floorboards creak when no one is there and the flickering candlelight creates shadows that creep along the walls. We truly wish we could tell you more, but we've been sworn to keep P. J.'s identity a secret . . . and it's a secret we will take to our graves!

Looking for another great book?
Find it
IN THE MIDDLE.

Fun, fantastic books for kids
in the in-be**TWEEN** age.

IntheMiddleBooks.com

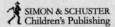
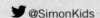